THIEVING FRENCHMEN

"Let's not start off playing games, okay?" Horne scowled, and drew his .45. "Give me my watch and my sixty thousand dollars."

"Monsieur, you have zee wrong man."

"Listen to me, Lucien DeBlois . . ."

"My name is Louis."

"Sure, and Lucien is your twin brother."

"Zat ees so."

"I'll give you ten seconds to open that safe before I blow your head off."

DeBlois opened it, and Horne saw a glint in the back. "My watch!" he uttered triumphantly.

Then the safe door struck the side of his head, sending crimson flashes through his brain. His skull exploded. Out he went.

T·G·
5
HORNE

DOUBLE TROUBLE IN SKAGWAY

PIERCE MACKENZIE

A SIGNET BOOK

NEW AMERICAN LIBRARY

PUBLISHER'S NOTE

This book is a work of fiction. Names, characters, places, and incidents either are the product of the author's imagination or are used fictitiously, and any resemblance to actual persons, living or dead, events, or locales is entirely coincidental.

Copyright © 1987 by Alan Riefe

SIGNET, SIGNET CLASSIC, MENTOR, ONYX, PLUME, MERIDIAN and NAL BOOKS are published by NAL PENGUIN INC., 1633 Broadway, New York, New York 10019

First Printing, August, 1987

1 2 3 4 5 6 7 8 9

PRINTED IN THE UNITED STATES OF AMERICA

1

He provided a singularly imposing impression in his custom-tailored broadcloth suit. His velvet vest was resplendent with hand-painted roses and violets in artistic profusion. From his broad-brimmed hat to his ruffled-cuff shirt to his Italian leather high-heeled boots, he was a living portrait of sartorial splendor. He fingered his diamond horseshoe stickpin and studied his thousand-dollar Jürgensen watch, its stem set with a single diamond, the timepiece itself moored to a four-foot chain.

The chain was neatly coiled and the watch leaned against a small hillock of velvet in the window of McCaskill's pawnshop. There T. G. Horne's Jürgensen had reposed on display ever since his arrival in Hurdlesford.

Like most western Kansas towns, Hurdlesford was not exactly a garden spot in midsummer. The incessant heat afflicted everything; life geared itself to a snail's pace. The residents floated like specters in a dream, going laboriously through the motions, as if conserving their energy for the cooler fall to come. Workers shirked and shirkers lolled about. Even the ceiling fans in E. W. Kelsey's saloon across the street circled so slowly they sliced the sultry air rather than stirred it.

Horne sighed as he studied his watch. He counted the fifty-two links in the chain—one for each card in the deck—and appraised his image in the window. Immaculately attired as usual, he could have passed for a diplomat, lacking only the cane. One might even mistake him for a nobleman, a haughty, imperious prince of the earth, but for his eyes. In them was a doleful, defeated look, a melancholy that clearly bespoke his dilemma. All the outward show of dignity, taste, opulence, and success could not mask his inner desperation. As his Jürgensen was stuck in the window, he was stuck in Hurdlesford. As a matter of principle he refused to leave town without his watch, and unable to redeem it, he could not leave, period. Day after depressing day he walked by the window, stopped to visit it, and walked on.

But not today. Into McCaskill's he sauntered, despising himself a little more with each step for what he was about to do.

"Mr. Richardson," boomed the pawnbroker. "Welcome, welcome. What can we do for you today?"

With this McCaskill rubbed his hands together vulgarly. His elderly face was as wrinkled as a prune; his corrugated smile overflowed his face, the ridges and crevices venturing up and over his bald plate, down his neck in the rear, and ending at his celluloid collar. In Horne's book the man was a miserable miser, a Fagin capable of squeezing the last dollar out of a defenseless widow, robbing a blind beggar's cup. Here was a man who could spot value at twenty feet through his nearsighted eyes and argue the deal to his advantage every time.

Horne showed him his diamond horseshoe stickpin. McCaskill fairly snatched it from his hand to examine it under his loupe. He hummed obscenely as he studied it.

"Real diamonds," he acknowledged. "Tiny, though, infinitesimal."

"But look at the purity. Not a carbon speck, not a gas flaw in the lot."

"Two hundred."

"Two . . . !" Horne gasped, swaying slightly in shock

that was not pretended. "It cost me twenty-five hundred originally. Look at the workmanship, the design, the beauty!"

"Three."

"One thousand dollars."

McCaskill handed it back.

A sinking feeling seized Horne's maw, dragging it downward toward his vitals. "Eight hundred," he mumbled.

McCaskill leaned over the glass counter and leered the leer of one in total command of the situation. "Not interested, son. I got half a dozen just like it, most of 'em better lying in the drawer. No room in the window."

"Six hundred and that's my final offer," declared Horne.

"That's *my* line, son." He stood staring at Horne. "You know, you're lucky. I like you. You're smooth, suave, cultured, and down on your luck. You have my sympathies. Four hundred cash."

"Deal."

McCaskill began counting the money out of a Blackstone cigar box that looked to be holding between six and seven hundred. Why, wondered Horne wearily, did all the wrong people have the bulk of the world's money? God knows McCaskill never did anything with his, least of all enjoy it. All he did was collect and count. His clothes were cheap and shabby, his glasses mail-order, his dentures ill-fitting and plastic-looking. He smoked not Blackstone cigars but two-cent stogies. He wouldn't give a starving man directions to a crust of bread, and yet he was disgustingly wealthy.

"There's no justice, none." Horne mumbled softly.

"You say something?"

"No." He watched him finish counting out the four hundred and thought of Pericles Jubal Youngquist, his uncle, the good Samaritan savior of this dirt-poor farm boy. Perry had taken him under his wing when his mother died and raised him as his own. He taught Horne all the myriad tricks and techniques designed to separate the unwary and overconfident from their money with a deck of cards. Perry was always there when T. G. needed him, though not lately. Were he to show up in Hurdlesford, he would cheerfully and unhesitatingly stake him two thousand dollars to redeem his watch and stickpin and get him back on his feet into a game. Two thousand at 35 percent interest, to be sure. Blood, though thicker than water, was not without its price.

His shirtfront felt naked without the stickpin as he emerged from McCaskill's. He had felt depressed before going in; coming out he felt so low he closed his eyes and pictured himself stretching to full height to peer over the top of a boot.

The need to dispatch his beloved stickpin to keep his beloved watch company pained him. Three months earlier he had been on his way to New Orleans. His thoughts winged back to that fateful game; a friendly game of seven-card stud in a clerestory-ceilinged private car, the epitome of Victorian elegance. Invited to join the game in Kansas City, he had been winning steadily until that disastrous hand, the one in a million capable of breaking a man's back and scattering the cartilage.

He had raised his monocled opponent only to be reraised. His hand, powerful, artfully disguised, a sure-fire winner, showed two pair: kings over deuces. Two of his concealed cards were also deuces.

Unfortunately, three of his opponent's concealed cards were threes. Combining with his one trey showing, they gave him four of a kind a single notch higher than Horne's four.

"Four threes," sang the monocle. "Beat 'em."

Stunned, in a fog Horne turned over his wired deuces, showing all four. The tension snapped, the kibitzers began buzzing and babbling, the monocle reached forward and raked in the pot. Horne retired from the fray, deserting the gathering badly shaken. He encountered the conductor in the vestibule of the car behind and explained his situation. The conductor was sympathetic;

he took back his ticket to New Orleans, refunding him $84.50, and sold him in its stead a ticket to the next stop: Hurdlesford.

Since arriving, he had gotten into a few games in the back room of Kelsey's saloon. And had lost steadily. So consistently, he shortly donned the cloak of a defeatist attitude; superstition also played a part. Before the first week was out he was beginning to believe that the tragedy of the four deuces was designed by fate to tell him he was finished—never again would be win with consistency, never again be so well-heeled he would squander his winnings on second-rate hands, confident that his luck would see him through to the pot.

The experience not only shattered his self-confidence and dispelled any semblance of optimism for the future, it drained him of his most precious possession, his courage. Now, whenever a promising hand came his way, he lacked the guts to bet it, and often fell prey to others' bluffing, which he'd rarely been guilty of before. He even hesitated to bluff himself when a bluff was called for.

Somewhere along the way he had lost his heart, or more precisely had pawned it along with his Jürgensen and stickpin.

His .45, Sharps .22 derringer, and Barns .50 boot pistol he could not pawn. Nor his dagger-mounted knuckle-duster. And despite the downward trend of his luck, he had to keep playing until it turned around. Three months—it couldn't go on like this forever; it had to end sometime. He sighed.

A three-piece band struck up "When the Roll Is Called up Yonder" at the corner. A comely-looking, fine-figured young lady in a black bonnet with a large ribbon tied under her dimpled chin was rattling a tambourine summoning passersby to listen to her sermon. A fourth man stood with the band holding a large vertical banner, maroon fringed with gold piping, on a pole proclaiming the Church of the Heavenly Calling.

Horne started up the street. By the time he reached the corner the lady preacher had gathered about twenty people.

"Is theah, ah say is theah anyone among y'all who can look into his haht and honestly say he has not sinned today?"

"I can," said Horne to himself. "Not yet at any rate."

"Y'all theah, young man. Ah'm talkin' to y'all."

"Me?" he asked innocently, the authority in her tone halting his step abruptly.

"You'h a sinner, ah can see it in youh hangdog look, youh shifty eyes that can't look me straight into mine, youh demeanor, youh air . . ."

"I beg your pardon!"

"Why, oh, why do ya'll sin? Why do you feel y'all have to? Has the Lawd been so unkind towahd y'all, so uncharitable and unfohgiving that y'all must elect the way of the transgressoh? What does Satan give y'all? Empty promises, false glory, fleeting success, lies, deceit and the oppohtunity to sin and sin again. Come ovah heah."

Despite himself, instead of walking on head down, avoiding his accuser's drilling eyes, he obediently approached her.

"Have y'all sunk so low that y'all can't reach up and touch the hem of the Lord's garment?"

Horne flared. "What is this? Who do you think you're talking to? What do you know about me? You've never even seen me before!"

"Ah have seen y'all all mah life, brother. In the dens of iniquity and sinful pursuits of the cities wheah evil flourishes and the devil sits in command. You'h a gamblah, aren't y'all? Admit it; y'all can't deny it, it's written all ovah you. Those clothes, that mustache, the sneaky, guilty look in youh eyes."

He could feel his cheeks burn.

"You mind your own god . . . your own business, lady."

"Correction, it's not my business but the Lord's. He

sees y'all as ah do, as we all do, a poor, afflicted soul strayed from the straight and narrow. Come to us, sinner, come to the Lord; leave the devil and the path of the transgressor; mercy and forgiveness can be youhs. Y'all need only reach out an' touch the hem of His garment to repent, to touch the stahs and redeem youh wuthless soul."

Horne walked on muttering to himself, the lady's tirade and her listeners' scoffing and disapproval ringing in his ears. He walked around the block, crossed the street, and started up it. Across the way the lady was lacing into another sinner, scolding and embarrassing him, humiliating him into changing his ways. He passed Kelsey's, glancing through the dust and pollen-scaled window studded with flyspecks and squashed insects. Two men footed the rail. The ceiling fans revolved as if under great strain, and he could almost see the suffocating air hanging in large chunks. He walked on.

"Mr. Richardson . . ." The bartender had come to the door, his knees pumping up his filthy apron, his face reddened and drenched with sweat from the heat, his gold tooth glistening in the sun. "Hold up a second."

"Basil," murmured Horne in greeting.

"There's a game tonight. New blood in town, so I hear. You interested?"

"Of course."

"Eight o'clock. Chapman and Browder came in about an hour ago to reserve the back room."

Horne's hand crept to his pocket. He gently massaged the four hundred.

"Who's the new boy?"

"Some Frenchman from the big city. He just got in this afternoon and was out looking for a game before his signature dried on the hotel register book, so Ollie Chapman says. And he looks like he's loaded."

"Does he, now? My, my . . ."

"He could be the pigeon you've been looking for, Mr. Richardson."

"Call me Alistair."

"Dropped from heaven into your lap to change your luck."

"Please, don't mention heaven. I've never felt farther from there in my life." Basil's expression clearly revealed that he didn't understand this. Horne went on. "Thanks for the tip. See you tonight."

"Eight o'clock."

Basil retreated, Horne went on his way.

With nothing but supper to occupy his time until eight o'clock, he wandered about town, ignoring the heat, savoring the possibilities of the impending game. It was about twenty minutes later when his steps brought him around the block to within sight of the corner where the lady preacher had earlier held forth, publicly insulting him. Her accompanists and her audience had fled the scene. Bandless and bannerless, she stood counting her contributions.

He crossed the street and went up to her. He was within two feet before she realized he was approaching, and looked up startled.

"You! What do y'all think you'h doing? Y'all scared the daylights outta me . . ."

"Forgive me."

"Foh y'all have sinned. Ah know, we been all through that."

Close up, she was even lovelier than he imagined: fresh, sparkling, her face without makeup, without any assistance whatsoever from bottles, tubes, powders, and paint. Lovely. And sensuous. Seductive, in complete contradiction to her calling.

"Don't you think you were a little hard on me when I came by before?"

"Don't y'all think y'all deserved it? How bettah to make a sinner see the errah of his ways than by holdin' him up to ridicule befoh his fellows? Shame him into changin' his evil ways."

"Do I really look evil to you? Do I? I wouldn't hurt a fly. I'm far from perfect, but I'm certainly not at the devil's disposal. Oh, forgive my bad manners, my name is Alistair Richardson."

"Emmeline Bagby."

"Permit me to commend you on your fierce dedication. You must be an absolutely spellbinder from the pulpit."

"Ah can only laboh with the tools the Lawd has given me."

His eyes fell to her figure. The Lord had given her a good deal more than most of her sex. He could feel the back of his mouth watering, and his organ twitched slightly as it awakened to the possibilities that encountering the lady promised. Horne turned his charm up to full power, laving compliments, interspersing heavily larded humility, downing himself, apologizing, humbling himself.

It worked. It generally did. Within minutes he broke her down, overcame whatever resistance her conscience raised in defense of her virtue, and got her smiling and staring invitingly. He offered his arm, she took it, and up the street they ambled.

It had always struck him as somewhere between curious and astonishing the way some women changed from the street or saloon to the bedchamber. The moment he closed and bolted the door behind them she began to disrobe. She was, he was delighted to discover, one who caught fire quickly. From the way she flung her things off, her mind, heart, and goodies were already in bed before her physical self.

She stood naked as a billiard ball before him, unselfconsciously unpinning her hair, letting it tumble free. She smiled and rolled her tongue from one corner of her mouth to the other. Then she came to him, undid his belt, unbuttoned his trousers, dropped them, and dropped with them. Seizing his slowly erecting cock, she encircled it with her hot lips and began to slowly suck.

Very slowly. Excruciatingly slowly. Magnificently . . .

In seconds she got him as hard as a cast-steel cold chisel, throbbing mightily, threatening to burst his balls and plaster her throat.

But just as he was about to ejaculate, she loosed her lovely mouth and stood up.

"Don't stop, don't," he pleaded.

She laughed a little, tinkling bell, and grasped his thick wet member, rubbing the purple head between the lips of her quim.

"I don't want it down," she explained, "I want it up . . ."

He tried to begin according to time-honored procedure: with foreplay. She immediately protested—wordlessly, electing to pull him bodily down on top, grabbing his buttocks, and driving his shaft root-deep into her. She began upthrusting wildly, pumping like an oversteamed pile driver, jamming her cunt against his helpless cock, all but driving it clear back through his belly to the base of his spine.

He speedily lost all sensation of body, desire, of the act itself. He was no longer flesh, bone, and sinew, but a large blob reduced to the consistency of jelly by her relentless assault. Never before had a woman attacked so savagely, so heartlessly, with such little regard for her victim. She seemed determined to destroy him. He could only hold his breath, hang on, pray, and await the inevitable climax.

She came, screaming at the top of her lungs in delight. He too blew, drenching the wet, pink cavern of her sex. Again she came, and a third time, and still she pumped and drove and bucked and pounded.

At last, limp as a boiled noodle, utterly exhausted, drained of every drop of energy, he freed himself and rolled to one side dead.

"What's the mattah, lovah, y'all huhting, tihed? Was it too much foh y'all? My stahs, y'all don't have a weak haht, do you?"

"It wasn't weak when we came in . . ."

"That's good news. Well, y'all gonna lie theah like a

dead catfish or are we gonna keep romping? I've foh keeping goin'; stoppin', restin' is foh weaklings. Ah like to romp, romp, romp till sunup and breakfast. Come on, lovah, let's get on with it . . ."

So saying, she jammed her mouth down on his limp cock and began sucking furiously, her head bobbing, hair flying, his cock slowly resuming erection, his balls boiling with fresh come. He sighed silently and closed his eyes.

And reflected: what a lovely way to die.

He was only able to get rid of Emmeline an hour later by pretending mortal pain and telling her his doctor had cautioned him against overdoing it in light of the poor condition of his kidneys. She left in somewhat of a huff.

He rested until suppertime, and when six o'clock arrived, he treated himself to a fairly expensive steak dinner with truffles among the trimmings and a decent bottle of imported burgundy. At seven-thirty, itching to get started, he stood at the bar in Kelsey's nursing a glass of Pitcairn Island French brandy and watching the clock. At a quarter-to-eight five men walked in: Ollie Chapman, a local grain merchant; his friend and business partner, Hedly Browder, Leland Cummings, a vice-president with the bank, and Alton Wheelock, manager of the local Wells Fargo depot. Horne had played all four previously and categorized them as good, fair, terrible, and exceptional in that order. Chapman had red hair and a matching mustache. Hedly Browder looked like an undertaker, and for that reason Horne had privately nicknamed him Deadly. Cummings was the picture of money and banking, from his silver hair and gold toothpick to his platinum-plated watch. Alton Wheeler looked like a cowhand out of uniform stuffed into a clean boiled shirt and Sunday suit. Red, Deadly, Banker, Cowboy.

The fifth arrival was the visiting Frenchman. He was introduced to Horne as Lucien DeBlois: "Deb-blow-wah, *monsieurs.*" Shaking his outstretched hand was like grasping a dead fish, although it was a large hand for the slender wrist from which it depended. It was also a hand that had never held a long-handled tool, had never worn a callus, and from fingertips to heel of palm was as soft and rosy-looking as a young girl's. DeBlois also displayed an expensive manicure, shining finger-nails, and a mustache that terminated at points as sharp as darts. His eau de cologne was either some kind of lily or orange blossoms; Horne couldn't tell which. The odor was not so strong as to attract questioning of his manhood and not so weak as to escape notice.

Horne shook his hand, inhaled his fragrance, stud-ied his mustache and face briefly, and decided on the spot that he did not like Monsieur DeBlois. It wasn't something about him, it was everything. A lace hanky was stuffed up one sleeve and at least once nearly every minute out it came to daub nonexistent moisture from under his nostrils. He took the chair across from Horne. Basil the bartender broke a new deck of Bicycles out of its cellophane seal; Banker shuffled, dealt for the deal, and Red came out of it with a queen and the first go-around.

They were only three hands into the game when DeBlois began mouthing off. For some reason explica-ble only to him, he targeted Horne.

"Monsieur Reechardson, forgive my saying so, but zee front of your shirt looks hideously barren. You should have a pearl stud or steeckpeen of some kind. A well-dressed gentlemen does not wear a shirt weeth a flowered vest weeth no jewelry at zee front, is zat not so?"

"I've a pearl the size of a pigeon's eye back at my room, the gift of a lady friend, but every time I put it on it looks so ostentatious I end up going without it."

"I saw a most eempressive diamond horseshoe steeck-peen een zee pawnshop window zis afternoon."

Horne won the next hand with a pair of sixes, suc-cessfully bluffing both Cowboy and Deadly. He won without either calling him, so he was not obliged to show his pair. To his surprise and annoyance, however, DeBlois reached over and brazenly turned up both sixes.

"*Mon Dieu*, what a trifleeng hand to ween such a substantial pot. Astoundeeng."

Horne turned his sixes back over. Why he bothered to, he didn't know, but the gesture drew smiles from Red and Banker. And a leer from DeBlois. At this Horne bristled.

"Since you're a visitor to our shores, *Monsieur*, perhaps you're unaware that the winner who is not called is under no obligation to show his cards."

"He's right," said Banker.

"Gentlemen, gentlemen, how can you be so streect? Ees zis not a friendly game?"

"It is," said Red.

And playing it like gentlemen was the best way he knew of to keep it friendly, thought Horne.

DeBlois proceeded to break practically every small rule of ethics in the poker book, feigning innocence in so doing and donning a pained expression when one or another player called his attention to his gaff. Everything he did was calculated to increase his chances of winning. He did not attempt the same trick twice and yet seemed determined to test the others' boiling points one way or another, particularly Horne's. He hadn't liked the man when he sat down, so now his efforts at minor sharking irritated Horne out of all proportion to their harm. DeBlois would look at his cards when they fell to him and, when the betting came around, would declare that he was betting in the blind. In a hand of stud he asked to see another player's folded hand and, when refused, brazenly turned the cards over. When Banker, the man who'd dropped out, took umbrage at this, DeBlois laughed it off, advising him to "be a good sport; we are all friends here." When, on the other hand, he dropped out he would immediately go rabbit-hunting, poking through the undealt deck to see what he might have drawn had he stayed in.

On three occasions he was caught paying short into the pot. When he lost, he sulked. When he won, he gloated boorishly and needled the loser. Curiously, no one else at the table seemed to mind either his behavior or his minor sharking as much as Horne. What really galled him was that DeBlois played the game very well and actually had no need to cheat or slow up the game with his shenanigans. He recognized the value of a given hand, saw the possibilities, knew the odds, knew when to stay, when to drop.

What he did not know was how to behave like a gentleman in the company of gentlemen. He was also snide, time and again lapsing into sarcasm and laughing at his observation when no one else would. He was also a bore, regaling them with tiresome tales of his adventures in the world of international finance.

The inevitable came about at the beginning of the second hour of play. He and Horne found themselves head to head in a hand of five-card stud. Horne had caught wired sixes and suspected him of wired nines. When, on the fourth card, DeBlois pulled Horne's six and began his needling, Horne came perilously close to losing his temper. When the case six fell to the Frenchman on the final card and each boasted a pair, Horne's annoyance began edging toward outright hatred. When, following the final bet, DeBlois turned over his hole card, a king, giving him the pair king high, beating Horne's pair ten high, DeBlois began laughing so loudly tears filled his eyes. Horne was tempted to lift his pantleg, draw his Barns, and put the ball squarely through his face.

"I don't see what's so funny," said Cowboy. "One man outdrawing the other in five-card is just luckier, that's all."

The others, excepting Horne, who was too upset to unclench his teeth, agreed.

DeBlois disagreed. "Eef he had bumped me at zee

first and second cards, I would have dropped out. He would have taken zee pot. He lost because he deed not have zee courage to reesk; I won because I had both courage and patience. Luck had notheeng to do weeth eet."

Horne got even six hands later, outdrawing him to aces well hidden and full in seven-card stud. The shoe now firmly on the other foot, DeBlois sank into a quagmire of gloom, bemoaning the fates and complaining about his rotten luck. What he evidently failed to notice, certainly failed to concede, was that Horne had cleverly kept him on the hook with little, seductive raises up until the fifth round. A less greedy player would have dropped out at the fall of the fourth card. Sheer luck alone brought DeBlois two helpful cards on the fifth and sixth rounds, whereupon he bet heavily, springing into the jaws of Horne's aces over tens. So he had no one but himself to blame for losing so much in a single hand.

But he did not lose consistently. By eleven, eyeing his stacks and rough-counting them, Horne estimated that DeBlois was ahead by some $28,000. He himself was up an equal amount. The big losers were Banker and Deadly, but both were taking their respective lickings gracefully, not at all like Horne imagined DeBlois would were he sitting in a losing chair.

Eyeing DeBlois' stacks and his own, Horne thought about chips and Perry's astute observation regarding them: "The man who invented gambling was bright, but the man who invented chips was a genius." How sage and how true. The chip was like a magician's sleight-of-hand that turns an orange into a rubber ball, a necessity of life into a plaything. People who hesitate to break a fifty-dollar bill in a store will toss a handful of chips totaling twice that amount into a poker pot with reckless disregard for the condition of their pocketbook or the odds. It was for this reason that poker was rarely played with cash. It was hard for inferior players to turn loose money, but using chips, they're hypnotized by the game. One point he and Perry agreed wholeheartedly on: in order to play high-stakes poker, one had to have a total disregard for money. You must look upon it as an instrument to be noticed and regarded only when you run out of it.

It was nearing two A.M., the quitting time agreed on before the first hand was dealt. Horne was nearly $30,000 to the good with DeBlois second to him but well behind. They were the heavy winners. None of the others was even ahead, and Banker and Deadly had both continued to lose consistently and heavily. There comes a point in every game when the heavy loser must stop and take stock and ask himself if his luck is ever going to change for the better. If he's smart, he'll tell himself no, fold his tent, and wait for the next game. But this did not seem to occur to either Banker or Deadly and they continued contributing to the winning hands.

The last deal fell to DeBlois.

"Let us play hold'em," he announced. "No leemit."

Horne stiffened. He had nothing in particular against the game, apart from the fact that generally the winner needed less skill and more luck than in other forms of poker. But the fact that the Frenchman suggested it indicated that he was not only experienced at it, but successful. His dark eyes covetously falling on Horne's stacks cinched these assumptions for Horne.

Hold'em is a seven-card game in which each player is dealt two cards and there is a five-card center. Basically a variation of seven-card stud, hold'em is nevertheless unlike any other kind of poker. It is crammed with action, much bluff, and usually, surprisingly low winning hands.

DeBlois dealt two down cards to each player. Horne looked at his. Seven and deuce. The two worst cards in the deck. He was tempted to fold immediately, but it was the last hand and he had won three out of the previous four pots. Why not push his luck a little, just to see how far it would stretch?

"One hundred," said Banker, sitting on DeBlois' left.

Deadly stayed. Horne raised four hundred. Cowboy and Red dropped. DeBlois raised an additional four hundred. Banker and Deadly dropped. Horne called.

"Ahhh," purred DeBlois, "zee ardor for zee raise ees suddenly cooled, eh?"

He turned over the first three cards of the flop: seven, four, four, giving Horne two pair.

"One thousand," he said quietly, and pushed his chips into the pot. Before he could remove his hand from them, DeBlois' shot toward his own stacks. Horne tensed. He had made a mistake. DeBlois' eagerness to bet gave him away; he had to have a big pair in the hole.

"Twenty zousand,' and DeBlois. Gasps ran around the table. Horne swallowed his own. The Frenchman yawned and smirked at him.

Horne considered the situation. His most logical move would be to fold. He was beaten. At this point. Only a bluff could save him. And this one hand must be saved. He could not let him take it; he must be denied. And it was solely up to him to deny him.

He called, knowing that if it did nothing else, it would instill doubt in the Frenchman's mind. DeBlois turned over the fourth card in the center: a deuce. It paired Horne's second hole card but did not improve his hand, since there was already a communal pair of fours in the center.

"Five thousand," said Horne, and pushed the chips forward.

This totally confused DeBlois. Doubt had clearly set in. He studied his depleted stacks. He studied the center of the table; he studied the back of Horne's hand, his chips, his face. And Horne noticed that his cheeks had paled ever so slightly, as if a bright light out of nowhere had suddenly been focused on them.

There was a long, long silence while DeBlois considered the implications of the bet. He had previously bet two-thirds of his holdings to knock Horne out. Not only did he fail to, but here he'd come back with a bet so healthy it reduced his chips to just a few.

Horne leaned forward, smiling affably.

"I have a suggestion, *mon ami.*"

"*Quoi?*"

"A suggestion. You give me a twenty-dollar chip and I will show you either one of my down cards. Whichever one you choose."

Another gasp traveled around the table followed by a circle of questioning frowns. Horne repeated his offer. DeBlois gazed at him with hate-filled eyes, and finally tossed over a chip. He pointed to Horne's top card, facedown in front of him. Horne turned it over. A Deuce.

Another long, electric silence.

The one, the only logical explanation for Horne's offer was that the two cards in front of him were the same, so the flop gave him a full house, deuces over fours. DeBlois weighed all possible considerations, arrived at the one, most logical conclusion, and folded his winning hand: three fours.

The game was over. Horne quickly scooped up the cards and squared the deck. No one, including DeBlois, would know that he had won with a bluff.

"Deuces full, right?" asked Banker.

"Right," said Horne.

Rapid mental calculation put his winnings at close to $60,000. As Perry so often said, When the worm turns, it spins.

2

Winning, in doing so destroying DeBlois, was delightful. Horne overflowed with joy and satisfaction, walking on air out to the bar, stopping by to reclaim his .45 and .22 Sharps. Perry would have been proud; he was himself. To win is delicious; to win with a bluff was heavenly! He had supped with the gods this night.

He stood in front of Kelsey's, lighting a Jersey cheroot, drawing on it contentedly, and reveling in his triumph. Banker, Red, and the others came out after him. They congratulated him and bid him good night. DeBlois was the last to emerge, bringing his plastic leer and floral scent with him.

"Lucky fellow," he murmured between tightly clenched teeth.

"Mmmm," responded Horne, feeling his chest on the verge of bursting with exultation, at the same time wondering how he might rub the Frenchman's nose in it. Still, that would be adding insult to injury, a posture beneath him, regardless of his dislike of the man.

"We shall play again, no?"

"Tomorrow night, hopefully. You'll have a chance to win it all back."

"I intend to *mon ami*. I shall. Do you know why?"

"I'll bite."

"Because I am a better player zan you. Class weel eventually tell, does eet not always?"

"Always. Witness tonight. Good night, *monsieur*."

DeBlois' expression when Horne waved and turned from him, setting his course for the hotel two blocks up the street, was that of a man intent on doing painful bodily harm with his bare hands. He was livid, seething with frustration. In his frame of mind he could easily murder. Horne hurried his pace, patting his .45 in its holster under his jacket, reassuring himself of its presence. The lady preacher, her critical barbs, brass band, and audience were long gone. Hurdlesford slept under a sky punctured with stars and the moonlight washed gleaming across the cobblestoned street.

First thing in the morning he must redeem his watch and stickpin, yet a another triumph in the offing. McCaskill would be so surprised he'd be speechless. Horne walked by the pawnshop. Both watch and stickpin were displayed in the window. How on earth had DeBlois connected him with the stickpin?,he wondered. Had he followed him into the shop and inquired of McCaskill? Hardly; when he himself left the place, the Frenchman wouldn't have had any way of knowing he'd be in the game that night.

What a body blow he'd delivered him. He looked to be still staggered when he walked away out front to Kelsey's. Horne shot a look behind him; no one was following. DeBlois appeared to have walked off in the opposite direction and no one else was abroad at such a late hour.

No one was manning the front desk when he entered the hotel lobby. And the lobby itself was deserted, smelling vaguely of furniture polish and stale cigar smoke. He hurried up the stairs, his step lightened by the joy in his heart and the sudden restoration of his long-absent self-esteem. He unlocked the door, went to the window to raise it to admit fresh air, then sat on the bed, got out his money, and counted it.

In six hours he had managed to turn the $400 given him by the pawnbroker into $60,040. What a bundle!

What a lovely sight, neatly stacked in fives, tens, twenties, and fifties with a fistful of ones set to one side. He would take a leaf from Perry's book and bank half to live on and gamble with the other half.

Dear Perry. Where was he? Still in San Antonio or on his way here? Thoughts of Perry, as always, brought on thoughts of home and his childhood. Oklahoma, its grayest, most dismal, most godforsaken area. His father had been a farmer who failed so consistently to bring in a corn crop, who brought a losing battle against the elements and the banks that never seemed to end, and who died trying to win and never came close. They had been dirt-poor every day of his childhood, had owned nothing, had been in debt for years—ever since Horne could remember. With the death of his father he and his mother had gone to live in the poor-house in Ada. Perry had come to their rescue, but within weeks Mother died and the twelve-year-old orphan was left to Perry to raise.

And raised him he had, sending him off to school with boots shined and hair slicked, sending him to Sunday school, although he himself never went near a church. Perry had introduced him to the mysteries of gambling, chiefly poker, when Horne was in his teens. Poker was, in Perry's view, the only game worth mastering. With its infinite varieties it was five-hundred games, and was perhaps the only game where a player may hold bad cards all night and still come out a winner. For Perry saw poker as a game of money management, not card management. In it there was a correct technical play in every situation, which the player, if he wishes to win consistently, must know. He must go even further. He must deliberately make the wrong technical play often enough so that his opponents will never be sure what he is doing.

Bluff is the essence of poker. It lurks in every single hand of the game. Has he or hasn't he got what he wants me to believe he has? The classic bluff was in five-card draw when you raise the opener, take no cards, then bet the maximum on your pat hand.

Has he got it or hasn't he?

Tonight's bluff, which filled his bed with money, was unusual: daring, impulsive, conjured up on the spot to meet the occasion. Devastatingly successful. DeBlois had hammered him with a twenty-thousand-dollar bet, but hesitated to add another five thousand—needing to pull light to do so—in the face of the doubt and uncertainty he, Horne, had so skillfully thrust into his mind. Offering to show him one of his two down cards was the pièce de résistance, the crusher. Once he saw the deuce his uncertainty triggered the conviction that it was one of a pair. He had folded, bluffed out of the biggest pot of the night. And till the day he died he would not know what his second down card actually was. To the day he died he would have to continue telling himself it was a second deuce. Were he to admit otherwise, it would so crush his spirit and conceit that neither would ever recover.

Sixty thousand and forty dollars.

Horne washed, dressed for bed, hung his clothes up, draped his six-gun and belt over the back of the chair, lay down, and still savoring his triumphant, his heart warm in his breast, his soul at peace for the first time in months, fell asleep. The breeze blew the white-aged-yellow curtains inwardly, the stars pulsed in the heavens, the streets of Hurdlesford stretched silent and empty in every direction. Two rounded pieces of wood eased out of the darkness and came to rest on the windowsill. A man stealthily ascended the ladder, reached the fourth rung from the top, and with delicate, slender hands lifted the window fully open.

Into the room he came, prowling like a shadow in the darkness. Pausing beside the bed, he lit a match. The scratching sound awoke Horne. He had been sleeping on his side, his back to the flaring match. He stirred, cleared his throat, and started to turn over.

Out of the blackness the butt of a .45 materialized in the grip of the intruder. Down it came, squarely against the back of Horne's head. Down he plummeted into a swirling pool of black.

3

Horne awoke with a headache that flooded his skull and descended his spine all the way down to his tailbone. It was slight outside, sunlight flooding the floor. Somebody was at the door; the knocking had awakened him.

"T.G.?" called a familiar voice.

He threw his feet over the side and stood up, bringing his suffering head up with him, locking his fingers at the top to keep the pain from erupting through his pate. Down he sank.

"T.G.?"

"Just a second."

The deliberately restrained volume of his own voice was still loud enough to send twin darts of pain shooting into both ears to join the aching inside. He took a deep breath and felt nauseous. Again he tried to get up, managed to, and stumbling to the door, unbolted and opened it. There stood a familiar figure: a magnificent mane of snow-white hair framing distinguished features dominated by piercing blue eyes that resembled chunks of ice and a patrician nose. Pericles Jubal Youngquist, the Solomon of sharpsters, the delinquent septuagenarian, looked like a giant grackle in his jet-black broadcloth suit and cloak with wide-wing collar. In one hand he held his floppy brim hat; in the other, his alligator skin club satchel.

"You took long enough. Great Caesar's ghost, if you don't look like the wrath of Jehovah and the heavenly host together. Look at those eyes, that rotgut is going to put you in an early grave, my boy."

"Oh, shut up. I wasn't drinking. Somebody sneaked in here and clobbered me." He cast about and his face fell so sharply one watching it might well imagine it made a sound. "And took my money, of course. Damn nation one and indivisible!" His eyes narrowed as he glowered. "And I know who! That disgusting, loud-mouthed, sore-losing frog Lucien DeBlois sneaked in here, bashed me over the head, and stole sixty thousand."

"Sixty—"

"And forty dollars. I counted it four times before I went to bed."

"You saw this fellow hit you in the dark?"

"I saw nothing."

"Then . . ."

"I smelled the son of a bitch." He sniffed. "Can't you smell it? Some floral scent, I don't know exactly which, but he was wearing it last night."

"I can't smell a blessed thing. Could it be your imagination?"

"Horsefeathers? I smelled it just before I went under. It's still here; faint, I'll admit . . ."

"Nonexistent is more like it." Perry eyed him worriedly. "You'd better sit down before you fall down."

"I've got to get dressed, get out of here, go and track him down."

"Are you serious? You really think he's still in town?"

Horne held his head between his hands, striving to wince away the discomfort. "Wait a minute. Basil the bartender mentioned that Ollie Chapman, one of the other players last night, said DeBlois was staying in a local hotel. There can't be more than two or three in the whole town. He could have been registered here. Let's go downstairs and ask to see the book."

"How about washing your face and getting dressed first?" Perry's glance had strayed to the open window.

"What on earth is that?" He walked over to it. "My word, you're quite right, T.G., you did have a visitor last night; he's left his ladder. But see here, you'd better be very sure before we go around town hurling accusations."

"It was DeBlois. I smelled him, I tell you. Nobody else in the game wore any cologne. And he's the one I clobbered."

"So he clobbered you. Tit for tat."

"Oh, shut up!" Horne washed his face a lick and a promise and dressed hurriedly.

"He took all your money?" asked Perry.

Horne checked the contents of his wallet. "All except this eleven dollars and change."

"You left sixty thousand in plain sight?"

"On the dresser. I didn't think somebody would climb in the window and steal it. I locked and bolted the door."

Perry still stood at the window. He leaned out and looked down the ladder. "You should have taken a room on the third floor. This ladder would never have reached."

"Funny. Let's go."

The desk clerk obligingly showed Horne the register. He flipped back a page.

"Here it is, L. DeBlois. Skagway?"

"Mr. DeBlois checked out early this morning," said the clerk. "He was in a grand rush. I think he was trying to catch the seven-fifty train."

"T.G.," said Perry, "you're not thinking what I think you're thinking, you're not going after him."

Horne did not answer right away. Instead, he closed the book, thanked the clerk, and taking Perry by the elbow, steered him to a far corner.

"He stole sixty thousand dollars. Added to which I don't like him. He's a first-class pig."

"He's also long gone. Be smart, my boy. Don't let

your emotions run away with you. Write it off as hard luck and forget about it."

"Perry, the luck I had last night was my first good luck in more than three months. I have suffered through the roughest summer I've ever seen. I beat him fairly and I can't let him get away with this."

"Skagway. My God that's a million miles from here. From anywhere."

"I don't care, it's the principle of the thing."

"What are you going to use for money?"

"I—"

"Eleven dollars and change won't take you far. Apart from which you have no way of knowing if he's heading for Skagway."

"It's his home base. Why else write it in the book? Certainly not to trick me. He registered yesterday. There's no way he could have known he'd be beaten in a big hand, walk away the big loser, and have to sneak into somebody's room and bash him over the head to get the money. No, common sense says Skagway is legitimate. There's a way to check it. Let's go over to the train station."

"Wait, wait; again, what are you going to use for money?"

"I, ah . . ."

"Would two thousand help? At the usual thirty-five percent, of course."

At mention of the two thousand dollars a smile started around Horne's mouth; at mention of 35 percent interest it vanished. He was left wondering why he'd actuated it in the first place, knowing as he did from experience that it couldn't last. Perry's inevitable next few words would banish it.

"Bloodsucker," he grumbled.

"Don't be harsh. Business is business. Take it or leave it."

"First let's hit the railroad station."

"My boy, why so glum? Your bird has flown, accept it. Or is it the interest?"

"I'll tell you what it is, I didn't pull a fast shuffle or peek at a bottom card or false cut or hold cards out all night. I played it straight as a die and won honestly. I—"

"Shame on you, after all I taught you, the hours, the practice . . . The bard was right: how sharper than a serpent's tooth is an ungrateful—"

"Oh, shut up!"

"He smelled of orange blossoms. I know because my wife uses the same cologne; I hate it." The ticket man peered over his spectacles through the vertical brass bars at them. "I sold him a ticket to San Francisco."

" 'Frisco," said Perry airily. "Not north after all—pity."

The ticket man was scratching his sparsely haired scalp. "Hold on. I remember; he first asked for a ticket through to Seattle by way of San Francisco. I told him there was no such animal. Best I could do was get him out to San Francisco and he could change lines there; work his way up: the Southern Pacific, the Northern, the Oregon-Washington line."

"Thank you," burst Horne, "thank you very very much."

"Think nothing of it, son. You boys want tickets?"

Horne nodded. "We have to get our luggage and tidy up a few loose ends; we'll be back. What time is the next train?"

"Forty-three minutes."

On the way back to the hotel to check out they stopped off at the pawnshop. Horne greeted McCaskill effusively and introduced Mr. Benjamin Marblehall, Esquire, a visiting friend. They stood surrounded by hanging musical instruments and glass cases crammed with merchandise, each piece either white- or pink-tagged.

McCaskill's greeting in response to Horne's was somewhat restrained. Horne could not think why. He asked to redeem his Jürgensen and diamond stickpin.

"Correct me if I'm wrong, the total was nine hundred. Plus your fee, of course."

McCaskill shifted his eyes back and forth, back and forth between them. He was beginning to look embarrassed.

"Ah . . ."

"You still have them," exclaimed Horne. "You didn't sell them . . ."

"Less than an hour ago. I opened at seven-thirty as usual. Customer was waiting for me at the door. Well-dressed chap carrying a satchel. Foreigner. Spanish or French, I don't know. In a devil of a rush. Paid cash, no haggling; he was out of here in two minutes."

Horne's face had gone white; his eyes swam in their sockets like a crazy's man's; he didn't speak, couldn't get his larynx to work. A series of soft sounds like those that might come from a wounded small animal issued from his throat.

Perry laid a comforting hand on his arm.

4

Horne sulked all the way across Colorado over the Rockies to Salt Lake City. Boarding the train in Hurdlesford, he sank into a foul mood, cloaking himself in bitterness and refusing to speak beyond monosyllabic grumblings and grunts in response to Perry's good-natured efforts to cheer him up. Perry finally gave up. They had been together, uncle and nephew, for more than twelve years and in all that time Perry had never known Horne to be so upset over an adversary's dirty dealings. A stranger assessing the situation would have imagined that Lucian DeBlois had been put on this earth solely for the purpose of destroying Horne's peace of mind, even dangerously threatening his will to live. The Frenchman's "pilferrings" of his watch and stickpin were, of course, the last two straws. To Horne they were more than jewelry; they symbolized his success in his trade, were emblematic of it. Not merely flashy gewgaws to set off his attire, but precious elements of his personality. Without them he was naked, a failure, on his uppers. With them, displaying them for all the world to see, he commanded his fate. He was in charge. Their presence on his person in a game imbued him with confidence, certain of his superiority over his adversaries. In the battle they were his sword and banner.

T.G. climbed out of the dank, dark burrow of his

depression with a windy monologue detailing all these points and others to Perry. Perry understood; he said he did. He also sympathized, but in expressing his sympathy, he slipped in a faux pas that stung Horne painfully.

"The irony of it is he redeemed your watch and your stickpin with your money."

Horne threatned to explode; Perry shrank from the sight and speedily placated him.

"But we'll catch up with him; we'll get them back. You'll see . . ."

Horne calmed down. "You're a true friend, Perry, even at thirty-five-percent interest."

"Listen to me, instead of sitting inside that black cloud all the way to the Pacific, come on out and play, why don't you? There's a game at the other end of the car: three drummers and what looks like a bank teller. Five-card stud. They could use a fifth man. What do you say, son? It'll do you good. You know, hair of the dog . . ."

Again Horne glowered. "I don't feel like poker. Especially when every dollar I toss into the pot has thirty-five cents riding on it."

"Ah, but everyone you take out of the pot helps chew up the interest. Come on, T.G., give it a whirl."

"Why don't you? You love five-card; I'll come and kibitz."

Perry eyed him. It was at least a start, he thought; it at least got him up out of his seat and doldrums and back in contact with the world. Horne led the way down the aisle. The conductor had supplied a board that the players supported with their knees. They had no chips and were using cash. Four strides from the game Perry whispered to Horne.

"We'll kibitz to start. I'll worm my way in."

They kibitzed. Horne watched in silence while Perry immediately began socializing: congratulating the winners, consoling the losers, feigning amazement at partic-

ular hands, complimenting the play. It took only a few
minutes before the door was opened to him.

"Care to sit in, old-timer?" asked a ruddy-faced man
in an inexcusably loud orange and brown plaid suit and
derby a size too small for him.

"Dear me," replied Perry taken aback. "It's been so
long I don't know as I remember the rules."

The man sitting alongside the man who'd invited him
in spoke up. He was blond and sunburned with miss-
ing front teeth and warts distributed about his hands.
"We'll teach you the rules, you just show us the color o'
your money."

Everyone laughed good-naturedly, including Perry.
The third player was a hairy individual in a crash linen
suit and New York straw skimmer. He stuttered slightly.
The fourth player was a beefy individual with a size-
twenty neck and fingers like sausages. Perry sat in.
Horne stood behind him so he could see his hole card.
Five-card stud was not his favorite poker game. He
played it, but did not enjoy it half as much as seven-
card and draw, nothing wild. It wasn't merely that he
fancied himself a purist, which he did, but that he had
long ago decided that five-card stud sparks real compe-
tition in only about one hand in ten. And when it does
arise, it is usually restricted to only two players. Essen-
tially five-card stud was much more of a gamble than
either seven-card or draw. The rules were simple. Dealt
a down card and one up, you do not stay unless you
have pair, unless your hole card outranks any card
showing, unless your hole card is the equal of any card
showing and your up card in a nine or higher.

Perry knew all the rules and never deviated from
them. Were he to win the twelve previous pots or lose
the same number, he would not break or even bend a
rule. Horne was more flexible, but could hardly fault
Perry's iron discipline in regard to rules in general. It
had, after all, consistently paid off for him over the
years. In five-card stud he dropped out on an average of
three out of every five hands; he refused to bluff. But

when the cards came his way he played them for all they were worth.

Within an hour in a two-dollar-limit game he was better than a hundred dollars ahead. Horne assessed the other players. None of the four appeared to know when to drop, perhaps the most important tactic of all in five-card stud. It did not seem to occur to them that when your opponent already has his ace and you are still waiting for one, he can get a second ace just as easily as you can your first. Moreover, with one ace already out, only three others are available, cutting your chances of getting one 25 percent. And high card wins at five-card stud with remarkable frequency.

Perry walked away from the game nearly $450 richer, strutting like a peacock up the aisle, Horne tagging behind.

"You should have gotten in, my boy."

"Not in the mood."

Horne took the window seat. Perry sat down beside him and began counting his money for the third time."

"Must you be so obvious?" rasped Horne irritably. "Put it away."

"Methinks I detect a note of envy in your tone."

He nevertheless pocketed his money. Horne got onto the subject of the fugitive.

"He touted himself as being active in international finance. What the devil would a financier be doing in Hurdlesford?"

"Why didn't you ask him?"

"I wasn't interested. Not then," Horne replied.

"More to the point, what's he doing up in Skagway?"

"Fleecing Klondike goldminers out of their claims and gold, no doubt. Cross your fingers we catch up with him before somebody puts a bullet through that plastic smile." Perry shook his head. "What's the matter?"

"This. Three thousand miles to retrieve your watch and stickpin."

"And my sixty thousand and my pride . . ."

"Has it occurred to you that if you get into a game on

this train, on the next one, on the northbound packet boat, you could probably win sixty thousand dollars before we arrive?"

"It wouldn't be the same and you know it." Horne paused to light a Jersey cheroot. They were crossing the Great Salt Desert of western Utah, the most arid and sparsely vegetated area in the entire Northwest: flat, dull, and blazing white. "What were you doing down in San Antonio?"

"Not to change the subject, eh? Renewing old contacts, making new ones. Setting the stage for you. Ah, me, two months down there and you could clean out Bexar County, every drop of oil money, every pound of cattle. There's nothing in this life that saddens the heart more than missed opportunity. Unless it's deliberately avoided opportunity."

"Bexar County will keep. Perry, do me a favor, indulge me. Quit complaining about my ringing you into this thing. Go along with me just this once."

"I'm going, I'm going. What am I doing here if I'm not?"

"If somebody swallowed you whole, chewed you up, and spit you out, you'd be just as determined to catch up with them."

"I only hope you do. I only hope this doesn't turn out to be the longest wild-goose chase in all our years together. What do you plan to do with him if and when you do catch up?"

"Wring my money out of him, reclaim my property, and burn him at the stake."

Perry grunted. "Just remember one thing, it's his backyard you'll be trespassing into. He's sure to have friends, he knows the lay of the land, he could very easily spot you before you see him, you can hardly inquire as to his whereabouts; your arrival is sure to get back to him before you can get to him. If you think about it, there's nothing that's not against you."

"You'll be there to help."

"No, thanks. Count me out. I'm not about to risk

getting my head blown off. We've been together too long. I'm just along for the ride, and to keep tabs on my investment. You really should have gotten into that game, my boy. This could have been your four hundred and fifty winnings. You could start paying off at least the interest on your loan."

Both were train-weary and stiff as sticks by the time they rolled into the City by the Bay. They took a room at the Plaza Hotel, squeezed between Burges, Gilbert, and Stills' publishing house and the post office and overlooking Portsmouth Square. From experience on former visits to the city they knew better than to accept when the desk clerk suggested a room facing the square. The din twenty-four hours around the clock was intolerable, and only the uninitiated and tightfisted took front rooms. While Perry napped, Horne walked down to the wharf and, after assessing most of the steam packets in port, purchased passage to Skagway on the *Charles E. Sterling*. Skagway lay about sixty miles beyond Juneau, itself nearly thirteen hundred miles from San Francisco. So shallow was the Skagway bay, oceangoing vessels had to anchor a mile from shore and passengers and cargo were ferried in scows and canoes across the mud flats at high tide.

Horne paid for their passage with Perry's money and was introduced by the agent to Captain Bairsford. The captain looked capable of wrestling a full-grown moose, and his voice and hearty laugh seemed to come up from his boots. An all-too-familiar gleam in his gray eyes suggested he had a strain of the flimflam man in his makeup. Horne mentally put up his guard.

Bairsford claimed his ship and made the run up to Skagway and back nearly four hundred times "without taking on a cup more water than she needs in her bilge. She's as safe as your mother's arms."

The *Charles E. Sterling* was the best of the bad lot in port at present; still Horne fleetingly wondered how any vessel so ancient could be safe. She was iron-hulled and, according to Bairsford, propelled by two one-thousand-horsepower engines. Horne knew next to nothing about ships of any type, but could see that she did not list from carrying too much bilgewater, her waterline stood reasonably high, and she had recently been put in drydock, her barnacles scraped and her hull painted.

"How many passengers?" he asked.

"Twenty-four, but we'll be taking a few more this trip. We make one stop: Astoria."

"How many more passengers?"

"All told, forty-four, and ye and your friend will make forty-six.'"

"That's pretty cramped, isn't it?"

The captain laughed and swung an arm the size of a railroad tie against Horne's biceps, sending pain flashing clear down to his wrist. "Ye' won't have to stand up all the way, if that's what's worrying ye."

"How long is the trip?"

"Seven days. Hop, skip, and jump."

"How's the food?"

"It's a pleasant, relaxing trip; the scenery's magnificent; the sea air invigorating; ye'll sleep like a log."

"How's the food?"

"Once the passengers get to know one another, it becomes just one big happy family. We've never had a single row, nothing worth writing home about."

"How's the food?"

"Three generous square meals a day."

"Edible?"

"Nourishing. Although it generally takes a couple days to get used to it. We sail at six A.M. sharp with the tide. Be here at least half an hour before. If ye'd like first-class accommodations . . ." He paused and rubbed his thumb against his fingers in the time-honored gesture. "I can see ye get the best damn quarters on the ship."

Never one to purchase a pig in a poke, Horne asked to see the first-class accommodations. They were tiny, cramped, with a single six-inch porthole to admit daylight, the door being louvered. He shuddered to think what third-class accommodations were, but turned over forty dollars for the stateroom and left. He reported back to Perry. When he was done telling him everything Captain Bairsford had told him, adding his own impressions, Perry sent him back out to the nearest pharmacy to pick up six packets of Cutshaw's Dyspepsia Pills.

Perry lay snoring that night; Horne lay awake staring at the darkened ceiling, listening to the muffled, distant clamor in Portsmouth Square at the front of the hotel. He rubbed the egg-sized bump at the back of his head and thought about Lucien DeBlois. He decided that, regardless of all this trouble they were putting themselves through, and with more to come, it would all turn out worth it. He certainly couldn't turn his back and walk away from the situation. He'd never be able to live with himself.

"I'm going to get you, Lucien, old boy. Get every cent back, my watch, my horseshoe, my satisfaction. I'm coming . . ."

"What if by the time we get there he's spent all your money?" asked Perry out of the darkness.

"I'll send him out into the gold fields to dig up the equivalent. That ought to ruin his manicure. One way or another, he and I will get square."

5

Perry was appalled at first sight of the *Charles E. Sterling*, until Horne drew his attention to some of the other steam packets at anchor, among them ancient side-wheelers and one disreputable-looking hulk scaled with stack soot an inch thick from bow to sternboard. Checking into their cabin, sight of which appalled Perry a second time, they were then summoned to breakfast by a bell. The main course was a bowl of lukewarm porridge as thick as molasses that tasted like wet cement and might have been put to better use sticking wallpaper in place. The meal was topped off by the vilest cup of coffee either had ever tasted. Perry took one sip, grimaced, and set down his cup.

"We're getting off this tub at once."

"Take it easy and face facts: this is the best we can do. We could hang around another six weeks and not do as well. Bairsford didn't say the food was edible, he said nourishing."

"To what, a goat?"

Horne looked up and down the table. All heads were bowed over their bowls, the diners diligently spooning up the thick gray substance. If anyone else found it unpalatable they weren't showing it. He resumed eating. The floor shuddered beneath his feet as the engines came thumping to life, powered by steam from the boilers turning the propeller, driving the *Charles*

E. Sterling through the murky water out of the fog-shrouded bay. Approximately four hundred miles to Astoria, the only stop en route. They would arrive there around midnight tomorrow, then on into the frozen north. Not exactly frozen, it being August and, according to Perry, who had it from an old sourdough friend years past, even winter weather was generally not severe on the coast. Although rain and snow were heavy and strong winds prevailed, the excruciating cold of the interior was unknown.

Captain Bairsford was right about one thing: the scenery *was* magnificent. The air was cool and clean, sweet to the taste. Horne and Perry spent most of the day on deck. After supper Perry downed two of his dyspepsia pills, voiced his regret at not having brought along a stomach pump, and they adjourned to the main cabin, where a poker game was in progress. Perry joined the five players already involved; Horne was content to kibitz. He evaulated the quality of play over the next hour and concluded that none of the five were tub-riders—Perry's expression for professional gamblers who make it a practice to ride public transportation up and down the rivers and coastlines. Many such individuals, caught cheating and banned from the Mississippi and Missouri stern- and side-wheelers, removed their skills and larcenous souls to the Pacific Coast to fleece unwary travelers aboard the steam packets. One of the five players quit at ten-thirty and Horne took his chair.

Seven-card stud and draw, generally with deuces wild, dominated the play. Betting was restricted to table stakes. By midnight Horne had won eighteen hundred dollars, Perry had even better luck, taking two enormous pots in a row, one with a small straight, the other with four aces, at least one of which Horne was certain he held out from the previous hand. Both abandoned the game at eleven-fifteen and retired for the night, Perry nearly $2,800 richer.

Neither of them played the next night, although the original five players did so. At twelve-thirty, while Perry slept, Horne was still awake, having not yet undressed for bed, when the *Charles E. Sterling* pulled into Astoria to deliver four bulging sacks of mail, two passengers, and take on three. The last passenger to board was a woman, the only female passenger. She carried a parasol and a blue-eyed, seal-point Siamese cat. The two men boarding carried her luggage for her. Horne happened to be standing at the starboard rail when she came up the gangplank. She was blond and quite beautiful; slender with impressive breasts, flawless skin, high cheekbones, and an imperious air.

She took one look at him staring at her, sniffed disdainfully, and looked away. When she walked by him, her cat on her forearms glared and hissed.

Perry's stomach began acting up early the following day, their third at sea. He forthrightly blamed the food, vowing not to consume another crumb until they put ashore at Skagway. Horne advised him to take a dyspepsia pill before his meal as well as after. And reminded him that they still had at least four days in front of them before Skagway.

"If you don't mind, I'd rather not have to carry you ashore."

The cook seem particularly fond of beef stew laced with kidney beans. Left with little choice, Horne quickly got used to it. Perry disdained the meat and picked out the beans, reasoning that even the most inept cook could not ruin beans. Horne passed the lady on deck numerous times throughout the day; he would smile, nod, and tip his hat, but all he got in response was an indifferent look and once a muted sigh, clear indication that she was finding him boring.

After supper, leaving Perry to retire early with his persisting indigestion, Horne wandered back to the main cabin and joined the game. Ten minutes after he sat down, the lady took the chair opposite him. Her cat sprawled on her lap. The cabin light did wonders for her beauty, showing her breasts in such a manner as to greatly increase their size and voluptuousness. Upon sitting down she stared through him and responded to his nod of greeting with a faint smile that might best be described as world-weary. To her right sat one of the original five players, a man in his late sixties, his heavily jowled face supporting a ludicrous-looking walrus mustache. He played, Horne knew, neither better nor worse than the other four. The question of the moment was, how good was the lady?

He had played against women before. Some had been most worthy opponents: good memories, excellent card sense, patience. Best without question had been Poker Alie Ivers, who had taken him to the trash heap on a train ride from Harlowton, Montana, to Fodder City, Wyoming, some years earlier. She sat across from him chomping on her cigar, not a particularly pretty woman, but—apart from her cigar—quite ladylike, demure. They had gone head to head in a hand of five-card stud. In that one hand she had taken him for a thousand dollars, inflicting irreparable injury to his bankroll and forcing him to drop out. She had outdrawn him, but up until the last card was dealt, he had had her beaten. His second card was a nine pairing a nine in the hole. She beat him with tens, adroitly keeping him guessing as to her hole card until the final disclosure.

He was holding his own in this game; he'd earlier decided he wouldn't cheat, regardless of how inviting the situation might be. His reason was that he and his opponents were all stuck on the vessel for the next four days. Were he to cheat and be caught, he could hardly draw his Barns, threaten his accusers, flee the premises, and ride off with his life. He therefore resolved to play it straight, and so he did well into the third hour. Then, with the lady dealing, they found themselves head to head.

The game was seven-card stud. Up until now he had not decided with any degree of certainty precisely how good she was. She hadn't won too many pots, nor had she lost many. She appeared to be playing conservatively and coyly, getting her cards and sitting on them until one of the other raised. At which point she'd practically throw her chips into the pot. She dealt him the ace of hearts and ace of spades in the hole, with three additional well-spaced spades among his four subsequent up cars. Giving him aces over nothing and a four-flush.

Herself she dealt the ten, jack, queen, and king of hearts up, drawing expression of wonderment and congratulations from the other players, all of whom save Horne had dropped out by the fifth card. At the fall of the sixth card, she bet heavily.

"One thousand."

He studied her hand. She could easily already have a heart flush, he thought. But not a straight flush. The walrus mustache on her left had dropped out on the fourth card, turning over the nine of hearts among his leavings. He himself held the ace of hearts in the hole, rendering a straight flush impossible. Moreover, only two other spades appeared around the table in the discards. His chances of drawing a fifth spade appeared every good. Equally important, he *felt* he could draw it.

"Call," he said.

Her cat stared at him insolently. He made a face at it in rejoinder.

"Last card," she said, and dealt him the seven of spades down.

His heart sang. He had the winning hand. Her slender hand floated out, grasped her final down card, and she looked at it. For fully thirty seconds before lowering it.

"King bets one thousand," she said coolly.

Horne studied his visible cards. Three of the four were spades: deuce, five, and ten. His ace of spades in the hole and the seven she had just dealt him gave him his ace-high flush. He studied her cards. Ten, jack, queen, and king of hearts. Eighty percent of a lovely straight flush. But never to be one. He held her ace, which would have given her a royal flush, and the nine reposed facedown in front of the walrus mustache, seated on her left.

"And a thousand," he murmured.

If anything it would teach her a lesson. Try being more selective when bluffing and don't make your opponent think you hold a card that he's already seen out of the hand. Excitement had erupted around the table. Everyone leaned forward expectantly except the lady and Horne. He had only about fifteen hundred dollars left. He would have loved nothing better than to reraise her, but the game was table stakes; besides, by now Perry was fast asleep; the bank was closed.

"Back to you," she said, pushing two thousand dollars' worth of chips into the pot.

"Call," he said quietly. He pushed forward his chips.

She flipped over her last card. "Straight flush, king high."

Her last card was the nine of hearts. His heart wrenched in his chest. She had cheated! Walrus Mustache had helped her, had slipped her his nine. Whatever she'd actually drawn for her final card was now either up her sleeve or on her lap under her damned cat. She stared at him stonily; then the suggestion of a triumphant smile began playing at the corners of her lovely mouth.

"Straight flush, king high," she repeated.

"Spade flush, ace high," he said quietly. "You win. Congratulations. That's it for me, tonight."

He looked over at Walrus Mustache. The man's eyes were completely blank, as if his brain had fallen asleep. Horne rose from his chair, cashed in his remaining few chips, and left.

"She cheated me, I tell you!"

"Did you accuse her? Did you accuse her confederate?"

"What could I say? If I accused either they'd only deny it. I'd end up looking like a sore loser with no way to prove what they'd done. That jowly old bastard with the outrageous mustache got on with us in San Francisco, didn't he?"

"He did."

"She got on in Astoria. Pretty slick."

"Not a new trick. Flimflam teams often do that to dispel suspicion."

"I'll get her, I'll get even . . ."

Perry lay in bed, supporting himself on one elbow. He stifled a yawn with his fist. He wasn't being sympathetic to Horne's plight; from all appearances he was finding it hard to generate interest.

"I'd be careful if I were you, she sounds to me like she knows her way around a poker table."

"What gripes me is if I'd won that pot, I'd have been able to pay you off, your usurious interest and all."

"I don't like that word, T.G. You're biting the hand that fed you. Cheer up, tomorrow's another day. Coming to bed?"

"Not yet. I'm too riled up. Conniving bitch!"

"Attractive-looking conniving bitch."

"I'll get even with her for this night's work or know the reason why."

"One or the other."

Horne snorted, grumbled unintelligible vile language to himself, and stormed out, slamming the door. He stood at the rail, the black forests of Canada slipping by a quarter-mile away. The sea was choppy, but the *Charles E. Sterling* had no trouble cleaving through it, sending water arcing up and outward from her hull. T.G. glanced to his right. She was standing at the railing without her cat. She noticed him, smiled, and came over.

"Beautiful night," she murmured.

"Lovely."

"Sorry about your bad luck."

"Luck . . ."

"I beg your pardon."

Her limpid eyes were suddenly suffused with innocence. He ignored it.

"The nine of hearts."

"I got it on the last card, weren't I lucky, though? That's all it was, out-and-out luck."

"Mmmm."

"Is something wrong?"

"Nothing. That was one healthy pot. I lost about twenty-seven hundred."

"This is absurd . . ."

"What?"

"Here I win all this money from you, we sit across from each other for upwards of three hours, and I don't even know your name."

"Forgive me, forgive my bad manners." He straightened and doffed his hat. "Alistair Richardson."

"Mr. Richardson." She offered her gloved hand. "Marion King DeBlois."

He could scarcely suppress a gulp. Could feel his eyes stretch. She frowned slightly, her own eyes inquiring.

"DeBlois?" he blurted.

"Marion."

"Forgive me, an old school chum of mine was named DeBlois. It's not very common."

"Not in the States. What was his first name?"

"Marcel."

"I don't know him; he's not a relative of my husband's. You're going to Skagway . . ."

"With my partner. Business."

"And what business?"

"I'm a schoolteacher by trade—semiretired. I've been dabbling in real estate. We're thinking of building a dance hall in Skagway if we can find a suitable piece of property."

"I'm sure you will. There's no shortage of land."

"You come from Skagway?"

"We live there, have for five years."

"Do you like it?"

"Oh, yes. It's an exciting town."

He sensed they were beginning to bore each other. DeBlois. Lucien DeBlois' wife—what an infinitesimally

small world. One good thing, he and Perry were headed
for the right place. Skagway was home for the thieving,
sarcastic, plastic-smiled blaggard. Perry would be relieved to hear it.

"It's getting colder," she murmured, and drew her
shawl more tightly around her shoulders. "I could use a
brandy. Won't you join me?"

Her cabin was nearly twice the size of his and Perry's; so much for Captain Bairsford's "best damn quarters on the ship."

She offered him a glass of Eau de vie de Marc, which
promptly dispelled the cold and bridled his rampant
lust for revenge against her. Oh, he'd get even, never
fear. God almighty; to think of it: cheated first by the
husband, then by the wife. It was incredible; it was
diabolical. One small step in the right direction of ven-
geance occurred to him as he sipped. She'd invited him
into the privacy of her cabin; she was sharing her brandy
with him; she had warmed up to him considerably since
the game.

Why not see what he could do in the way of installing
horns on Lucien's brow? Monsieur Lucien Cuckold
DeBlois. It had a nice ring to it. Did she play other
than poker? he wondered. He could see nothing to
prevent his finding out.

Still, better let her make the first move.

Which she obligingly did, during their third round.
She undid the four buttons above her décolletage and
undid his necktie and began to unbutton his shirt. Up
close she smelled deliciously not of orange blossoms,
but jasmine, so deliciously it set his senses swimming.
When she lowered her hands from his shirtfront, he
embraced and kissed her lightly. When she eagerly
responded, he kissed her ardently, then eased her down
upon the bed.

"I'm a married woman," she said gaily, smiling, and
took off her wedding ring, setting it up on the nightstand.

It was all the invitation he needed. He disrobed her

skillfully and speedily; she reciprocated even faster, her fingers flashing, releasing buttons and laces, and presently they lay side by side in the raw. He took her in his arms and kissed her hungrily, then started his mouth down her graceful neck to her shoulder and inwardly down one breast and up the other. Returning to her nipples, he laved them with his hot tongue, hardening them like rivets. She moaned softly and shifted her thighs. His hand eased down to her V and he inserted his finger and began titillating her clitoris. Again she moaned. Again and again he kissed her. She began moving against his probing finger, bucking onto it, swinging her hips. Her hand groped for his cock, already erecting.

"It's lovely," she murmured. "Firm, throbbing. Put it in."

"Soon . . ."

"Now!"

"Soon."

"Please . . ."

He held off, swinging his hips, pulling his cock gently free of her grasp, lest she so arouse him that he would come prematurely. Presently, he turned over, raised, and began slowly lowering. She took hold of his cock and set the head between her moist, warm lips, then gripped his buttocks with surprising strength, pulling him down, driving his cock deep.

"Ooooooo. Beautiful . . . ooooo, lovely."

He began slowly pumping, eliciting a litany of satisfied reactions. Now she was working up into a frenzy, driving upward harder and harder, bucking, gyrating wildly, her arms vised around him.

"Ooooooo," she moaned, and sank her teeth into one shoulder then the other.

They came together, thrusting violently. It was ecstasy. For fully ten minutes they did not separate; he continued to lie atop her, his limp organ thrust into her. Then he began to withdraw. She protested.

"Leave it in, please! Please! I'll make it hard for you . . ."

She did, much to his surprise, working it, massaging it with her cunt until rigidity was restored. Again they fucked, again came simultaneously. He lay in her a long time before easing free at last and rolling onto his back.

"I loved that," she purred softly.

"It was lovely," he said, and summarily dismissed all thoughts of her duplicity. He closed his eyes, envisioned DuBlois' face, grinning plastically, and saw horns protruding from his forehead.

It would all work out, he assured himself; he'd beat her at the table; he'd beat him in Skagway; physically and every other way.

Her cat, which she called Monsoon, stirred in its bed in the corner and came awake. Two icy blue eyes stared at him through the darkness. He tensed, imaging that it was about to spring, land on him, and naked as he was, scratch him to ribbons. She noticed that the cat had awakened.

"Here, Monsy, came to Mama."

Horne got up quickly and into his clothes.

"What are you doing? Where are you going?"

"I must get back to my cabin. My partner, Mr. Marblehall, hasn't been feeling well. I have to see if he's all right."

"Will I see you again?" She smiled hopefully, even worried, he thought, that she might not.

"Of course. We'll play tomorrow night, won't we?"

"Indeed we shall. Poker and here. Kiss me good night, lover."

6

The next morning at breakfast, which Perry sat down to only when Horne's insistence began to take on the sharp edge of threat, the older man raised a point regarding Marion DeBlois' cheating.

"She could have stolen that nine of hearts from the fellow sitting next to her without his even knowing."

Horne swallowed a spoonful of the glutinous mass in his bowl and considered this. "I don't think so. She couldn't very well fiddle with his discards in the midst of playing her hand. The way I see it she palmed a throwaway, put her free hand under the table, and he—knowing perfectly well what she needed—swapped the nine for it."

"There's a way to prove whether or not they are in cahoots. If they are, you'll have to keep one eye on him. If not, you can concentrate fully on her. Tonight when you sit in, I'll sit in. By the way, are you tapped out?"

"I've got about five hundred. If you're worrying about your loan."

"Great Caesar's ghost, what do you take me for? Of course I am. If she puts another one over on you tonight, she'll bust you and I may never see a nickel."

They spent most of the day on deck watching the magnificent scenery glide by. Among the masses of greenery stood grotesque whitened skeletons of lightning-

53

struck cedars, and now and then the great tall totem poles of the Tlingit and Kwakiutl tribes identified their villages at the water's edge. Deer and moose could be seen coming down to frolic in the water. And Marion DeBlois was seen, by herself as usual.

"She looks as innocent as the proverbial lamb," commented Perry. "How do you plan to even the score?"

"Whatever the opportunity suggests when it comes up. One thing's in my favor, I know she doesn't suspect I'm a pro. She'll be looking for some kind of move from me in retaliation, she'll keep her eyes peeled, but she won't see a thing."

"I can't wait for tonight." Perry rubbed his hands briskly. "I wouldn't miss this for the world."

"Perry . . ."

"Eh?"

"Ahem, talking about money, I could use about three thousand."

Perry feigned astonishment. "Three thousand dollars? What do I look like, the Bank of England?"

"You've got it; you'll get it back the second the game's over."

"I will if you win. If you don't . . ."

"Be sensible. How can I not win?"

"Stranger things have happened. All right." He fished three thousand out of a billfold so fat he could hardly bend it. "At fifty percent."

"Fifty!"

"Shhhh, you'll attract attention."

"You bloodsucker."

"Balderdash. You must know by this time that interest is keyed to urgency. You needed the two thousand in Hurdlesford; I charged you thirty-five. You desperately need this; I'm charging you fifty."

"If I don't return it immediately after the game."

"Precisely." He consulted his watch. "The time is now four-twenty-one. At four-twenty-two tomorrow afternoon—"

"Okay, okay."

The day dragged on leaden feet for Horne. It would have been all but unbearable had not chance placed him in Marion King DeBlois' path as she promenaded the deck.

"I've been looking for you."

"I've been right here on board," he said.

She lowered her head slightly, smiled demurely, and winked, holding her upper lid against the lower for fully three seconds. He got the message. She pressed her key into his hand.

"You go first, I'll be there in five minutes. Mustn't be conspicuous, must we?"

He swallowed nervously, his brain spinning, heart racing, blood surging, balls slightly burning, as if already beginning to charge up for the encounter. He made his way to her cabin, let himself in, undressed, and climbed under the sheet. Five minutes later she came in.

"My, aren't we in a hurry."

"Time's fleeting."

She sat on the edge of the bed, undid her blouse, and set his hand over her breast. It was surprisingly warm and the nipple already hard, poking insolently against his caressing palm. She took away his hand and slowly pulled the sheet down.

"What have we here?"

"First come, first served."

"How did you know I skipped lunch?"

Without another word she went down on him, chewing softly, gently, hungrily, then began sliding her lips up and down, up and down. Within seconds his head felt as if it would explode. His balls surged, roiled, and rang. Come rocketed up his channel and blasted against the roof of her mouth. She continued sucking without breaking the rhythm, devouring the last lingering drop. One had caught at the corner of her mouth. Out flashed her tongue, the tip capturing it, folding it inside. She smacked loudly.

"Delicious. I love sucking you, I love the feel of your

strength surging up your thing, capturing it from you, swallowing it, feeling its warmth in my tummy. Your strength becoming my strength."

Spare us both the philosophy, he mused. Can we go on?

Go on they did. Once again she sucked him hard, rid herself of her skirt and underclothes, and backed against the wall.

"Fuck me standing up. I like it."

"I aim to please."

"Aim straight . . . please."

He pushed slowly into her. She obligingly bowed her knees slightly, lowering to accept him and widening the port of entry for the *S.S. Horne.*

"Ooooh, that's delicious," she cooed. "Push! Push!"

She impatiently pulled him deeper, then began slowly revolving around his cock, employing it as a pivot to her passion, moaning, sighing. As she gyrated she rolled her eyes, sudden captive to absolute ecstasy. Her swollen tongue fell from her mouth and lolled back and forth. And she fucked until the sweat poured from her, her nipples threatening to rip through her flimsy blouse . . .

This, he reflected, was a woman born to fuck—and willing to give as good as was given her.

In the hour that followed they exhausted each other. They lay panting side by side on the narrow bed without speaking until she finally got up and dressed. He did also. She unlocked the door.

"Thank you, Mr. Richardson."

"Alistair."

"It was fun, we must do it again soon."

They shook hands and he left.

Back out on deck he found himself looking up at the pale sun and urging it to descend faster. When at last it set, turning blood red and depositing itself in the white-capped sea, he begin to undergo a marked change. Impatience yielded to psychological preparation for the night's doings; he began to gear himself mentally. He even repaired to the cabin to rub his fingertips with emery paper, as he did every morning upon arising to sharpen their sensitivity, enabling him to feel pinpricks in cards, bumps and ridges and strippers.

At eight sharp the players filed into the main cabin. Still intent on proving whether or not the lady and the walrus mustache were in cahoots, Perry tried to slip a chair between the two.

"I'm afraid there's no room here, old boy," said the man affably. "Try the other side."

For all his comical-looking mustache and pudding jowls, he was a courtly individual, soft-spoken and displaying traces of a flair that doubtless had made him quite stylish in his youth and attractive to the ladies. Perry did not insist on sitting between them, but the man's effort to discourage him proved Horne correct.

There were seven players. It was not until late in the first hour that Horne and the lady found themselves head to head. By now it was dark outside; the sea wind had come up, bringing cold and whistling plaintively around the smokestack. The deal was to the lady. She chose seven-card stud and promptly dealt herself a pair of tens in the hole, king up. A fair hand to start, she decided, but it could use protection. She looked across at Horne's up card: jack of hearts.

Another player, a gregarious and energetic little man seated on Horne's left, bet his ace. The betting came around to her.

"Raise two hundred."

Horne only called her. The others, including Perry and the opener, folded.

Walrus Mustache took the deal, shuffled; she cut, he dealt Horne the six of clubs and her the ace of hearts, giving her tens wire, ace, king up.

"Five hundred," she said.

Horne correctly read her hole cards as a pair. Of what, only time would tell. But at the moment, sufficiently strong to encourage some fairly heavy betting on her part. Around came the third up card; for Horne the seven of clubs; for her, the three of clubs. Ostensibly, no help to either hand.

"Ace, king check," she murmured.

"Check," said Horne.

The next round brought Horne the ace of hearts and her the eight of clubs. Again no help to either hand, but to Horne's surprise, she bet.

"One thousand."

He studied his cards intently.

"The spots won't change, brother," commented the little man on his left, drawing mild laughter from the others.

"Call," said Horne.

Last card. Down fell hers, down his. She lifted a corner: ten of clubs. Three tens. She kept her expression somber, the classic poker face. She raised her eyes to Horne as he checked his last card.

"One thousand," she said.

"Make it two thousand," said Horne.

Again her eyes fell to her cards. She could feel Horne's eyes on her. She tensed and stifled a small gasp. She had made a mistake. She had failed to notice that two of his up cards were hearts: jack and ace. So intent had she been on milking her tens and so elated at catching the third one, the two hearts in Horne's hand had not registered. Now she was trapped; she could not fold. He could be bluffing; she saw him as fully capable of it. And even if he did beat her, she would come back at him; the night was young.

She berated herself; not only had she not kept track of his up cards, she hadn't even counted the other hearts showing. She had made herself a voluntary victim of a snare even the best of players occasionally become entangled in: focusing her full concentration on her own cards, all but completely ignoring her opponents. It was a temporary lapse in discipline.

A costly lapse.

Horne flipped his cards over, revealing the queen and two low hearts. He reached for the pot. A voice called outside the porthole behind her. Thumping feet and shouting could be heard.

"Fire!" yelled the voice.

Bedlam erupted at the table, hands snatching up chips, chairs scraping the floor, players and the kibitzers alike bumping into one another in their haste to get out. Horne flew out, tugging Perry after him. The fire call repeated. Outside, both took one look shoreward and groaned in unison.

It was a fire. Raging. Onshore, majestic cedars were going up like tinder. Started not by lightning, for the weather had been uniformly clear since their departure; started more likely by a careless Indian cooking on the hunt. It was an awesome sight, a monstrous torch seemingly bent on firing the heavens. The passengers crowding the starboard rail caused the ship to list in that direction, and finally Captain Bairsford called everyone to attention and politely asked them to disperse and thereby distribute their collective weight more evenly.

Gradually the blaze slipped back beyond the stern, an effort was made on the part of a few of the more indignant passengers to ascertain who the damned fool was who'd yelled fire, making everyone think it was on board, and the card players drifted back to their game.

The third deal came back around to Walrus Mustache. Horne watched him shuffle dexterously and deal draw. Horne let all five of his cards drop before picking them up. He studied the backs. He squinted. Something was very wrong; he couldn't make out what it was immediately, but his instincts shrilled warning. While the other players began to pick up and arrange their hands, he continued to leave his facedown in front of him.

He lowered his head slightly, intensifying his squint. Then he picked up his cards. He had been dealt two queens, two small spades, and the nine of diamonds. But it wasn't the value of his hand that interested him. What he had discovered before he'd picked it up, checking and double-checking to make sure, fascinated him.

The deck in play looked to be the same deck they

had been using when the game was interrupted, provided by the captain brand-new, still in its cellophane wrapper. The design on the back was an inartistic clutter of clovers, figure resembling clovers, hash marks, angles, crosses, and solid and open circles.

This was not the deck.

This deck was readers: marked cards. About one out of every hundred decks sold was doctored. Expertly. He had seen marked cards with the identifying marks so skillfully hidden, the uninitiated could not spot them even after long, close study.

The key in this instance, which he had spotted and took the time to make sure he was not seeing things, was a dotted 7 in the upper-right and lower-left corners. The symbol revolved clockwise through eight distinct patterns as the cards increase in value from seven through ace. Different marks divulged lesser cards. Suits, less important than card values, were ignored. Walrus Mustache had introduced the deck.

Horne avoided looking his way, at the same time assuring himself that Marion DeBlois was in on the hanky-panky. He studied the backs of her cards over the top of his hand. He could make out an ace, a queen, and a ten.

The object of the deception, he knew from experience, was not to deal oneself a powerful hand, but to enable one to ascertain the value of the other fellow's hand. Marked cards were particularly helpful in seven-card stud, wherein three cards are always facedown and rarely cover one another throughout the entire hand.

He thought about shielding the back of his own upraised cards with his free hand, but doing so might betray his discovery of what was going on to the cheater. He decided to play the one hand without interrupting, just to see what would happen.

He studied his queens. The chance of improving them drawing three cards was only two in seven. Perry, sitting on Walrus Mustache's left, opened. Had he too spotted the readers? Horne wondered. Probably not.

His eyes weren't very good anymore, had gotten much worse over the past two years, and yet he still refused to invest in glasses. Fortunately for him, he didn't play that often. Horne's own eyesight was superb. He had no trouble reading almost every card facing him. It merely had to reveal at least one of the two marked corners.

When the betting came around to him, he dropped, preferring to watch. Perry had a strong hand. When the man sitting opposite him raised him and Walrus Mustache saw the raise, Perry saw and reraised. His opponent merely called.

When they drew their cards Horne studied each of the three hands in turn. Perry had three kings. The man who'd raised him held two pair: jacks over tens. Walrus Mustache held a small straight. Horne watched him angle his head awkwardly in order to get a good look at the backs of Perry's cards. He evidently saw enough to tell him what he wanted to know. When Perry checked and the other fellow bet one hundred, Walrus Mustache bumped him a hundred, bumping Perry out, and eventually took the pot with his four-to-eight straight.

He reached into the center. Out shot Horne's hand, seizing him by the wrist.

"I wouldn't if I were you," he said mildly.

Marion DeBlois was suddenly staring at him.

"I beg your pardon," rasped Walrus Mustache, and strained to free himself.

Horne held fast. "Don't take it. You've won it unfairly."

A gasp raced around the table. Perry was looking at him strangely.

"While we were outside watching the fire, you rang in a deck of marked cards."

The jowls quivered, the mustache bristled, the face reddened and trembled. "See here!"

"If I'm wrong, I'll apologize."

Everyone's attention was drawn to the table, Captain Bairsford joining the host of onlookers. Horne effectively screws Walrus Mustache to his chair with a threatening scowl, let go of his wrist, collected the cards, shuffled, and spread them in a long line facedown.

"Each one of you take a card."

All, save Walrus Mustache, complied. Horne pushed the remainder of the deck to one side and asked everyone to place his card facedown. He then proceeded to identify each card correctly from its marking. Ooohs, ahhhhs, and more gasping ensued. Captain Bairsford was the first to speak.

"Sir," he said, glowering at Walrus Mustache, "ye give me no choice but to put ye ashore at the next landfall. We're coming up on the Queen Charlotte Islands. We will put in at Cape Saint James and ye will disembark."

"I protest," shrilled Marion DeBlois, and ran a protective arm through that of the man at her side. "You can't, it's inhuman!"

"It's nothing of the kind, madam. He'll be perfectly safe there; there isn't a savage on the entire island. There are trappers; he'll be able to get passage to Astoria. There will be no cheating at cards on board the *Charles E. Sterling* while I'm master, and them that tries will have to pay the piper. That's all I have to say on the subject. I suggest, sir, that ye collect your things and be ready to get put ashore. We'll be there in less than twenty minutes."

"I'll go ashore with him," burst Marion.

"As you wish, madam, though you're not obliged to. No one is accusing ye of anything."

"This is all your fault," she shrilled to Horne. "Why don't you mind your own business?"

"I myself, and I'm sure your fellow players, are most grateful to Mr. Richardson," said Bairsford loftily. "I'll thank ye not to accuse him, I'll thank ye not to make a scene. Good evening, all."

Out the door he strode. The pot was properly divided among the three participants in the hand. Players and onlookers drifted off about their business. Horne and Perry went out on deck. They did not have time to begin discussing the incident when Marion DeBlois appeared. She looked to have calmed down.

"Excuse me," she said icily, "but I have to say that was a cruel and unnecessary thing you did in there to poor Mr. Kay."

"No crueller than he deserved, and very necessary. The rest of us in the game were playing honestly. He had no right trying to cheat; there's no excuse for it."

"My, my, my, but aren't we holier-than-thou all of a sudden. Don't try to tell me you've never bottom-peeked or held out cards."

"I've cheated, but not on this trip. Not once. Can you say the same?"

"Absolutely."

"That straight flush you beat me with last night was a four-flush until your friend Mr. Kay slipped you the nine."

"That's a filthy lie," she flared. "Why am I standing here talking to you, anyway? What's the point?"

"I wouldn't know, Mrs. DeBlois. I was hoping you might."

Her eyes gleamed with disgust; she was trembling she was so angry; her cheeks flushed; she started to respond, thought better of it, stamped her foot in frustration, and stalked off.

"Was that wise?" asked Perry.

"It was certainly satisfying."

"I should think you'd want to stay on the right sides of the lady."

"How the hell could I? What am I supposed to do, let him ring in a deck of readers and say nothing? Goddammit, Perry, if I can play it straight, so can they. Besides, what's the difference? I don't need her anymore. I won my money back; honestly, I might add. Here's your three thousand."

"Won back your money and affixed the well-known horns to the lady's unsuspecting husband's head."

"Not exactly. Technically speaking, I didn't bed her, she bedded me. She gave him his horns."

"Isn't that distinction a bit like splitting hairs?"

"Not to me."

"All the same, my boy, deliberately turning her against you was uncalled for. She might have come in handy up in Skagway."

"You're not thinking, Perry. An hour after we land there I'll be going after her husband. She'll find out the truth, I can't prevent it. She'll be on the other side of the fence from then on; so I put her there a little early. What's the difference?" He frowned pondering. "I wonder . . ."

"What?"

"You think she really intends to disembark at Cape Saint James with Mr. Kay? Or was she just spouting off? I hope she does get off; we could get up there and take care of our business before she even shows up. It'll be less complicated if she's not around."

The *Charles E. Sterling* dropped anchor off Cape Saint James a few minutes later. A dory was readied. Everyone assembled on deck to watch the departure. Mr. Kay was a pitiful sight: suffused with embarrassment, unable to look anyone in the eye. Mrs. DeBlois and the man assigned to row them helped him into the little craft. They settled in the rear seat. Horne and Perry stood at the railing looking down with the others. She sat facing them, wearing a long, voluminous cloak with a hood over her head against the chill, her cat in her lap. As the man rowing took hold of the oars, she looked upward at Horne. Her expression was one of stinging hatred. At the sight of her eyes he almost winced. She reached into her bag. Something shiny glinted in her hand in the lantern light. A gun. She raised it. Those looking down at her reacted in horror, shrinking from the railing. She was staring straight at Horne. Mr. Kay, seated beside her, thrust his arm upward as she fired. The bullet flew over Horne's head and to the right as he ducked. Kay wrested the gun from her and flung it into the water.

Away they went, the oars dipping softly, the dory gliding off, Mrs. DeBlois getting control of herself with Kay's help.

Perry shuddered. "He saved your life. You look pale, my boy."

"I feel pale."

By now all that could be seen of them was the small ball of yellow light in their lantern.

"Mr. Kay," said Perry ruminating. "Kay . . . What did you say her name was?"

"Marion DeBlois."

"Marion something DeBlois, wasn't it?"

"King."

"You don't suppose Mr. Kay isn't K-a-y or K-a-y-e, but just the letter K, short for King?"

Horne's eyes rounded slightly. "Father and daughter. No wonder she was so upset."

"It would explain her reaction, all right."

"Good lord . . ."

"Congratulations, T.G., on making yourself another formidable sworn enemy. First the husband, now the wife. I wonder if they have any children?"

7

It took better than two days more to come within sight of Christian Sound and the Channel Strait, which led to Juneau and up the Lynn Canal to Skagway beyond. The two nights Horne spent at the table in the main cabin were scandalously profitable. By the time he turned the last card of his hand on board, his winnings had risen to nearly four thousand dollars. He paid off his loan plus the interest and pocketed well over seven hundred. Uncle and nephew sat in the cabin after breakfast the next morning, Perry packing his belongings, Horne smoothing his fingertips with emery cloth.

"Enlighten me, my boy. What part am I supposed to play in this charade you're planning?"

"I need you to be my advance man. Track down DeBlois, get all the information you can about him. If he works, where he works, his comings and goings, where he lives; most important of all, when's the best time to catch him alone."

"Then what?"

"Then, just step aside. I'll confront him."

"And demand your money, your watch, your stickpin. And if he doesn't come through, what then? Will you shoot him?"

"Hardly. If he doesn't have the money if he's blown it all, I'll . . ."

"Yes?"

"I . . . don't know. I'll have to play it by ear. The one thing I'm sure of is I'm not leaving Skagway without it. What I'd really like to do is get square with him and haul him back to Seattle to stand trial. I can make a citizen's arrest."

"Don't be ridiculous." Perry paused in his packing and eyed him sympathetically. "My boy, I sincerely hope you get everything back, but if you can't, take my advice: don't stir up a big fuss. This is his home base. I'm sure he has many friends."

"I now, I've thought about all that. On the other hand, I didn't come all this way to go back empty-handed."

"Don't expect any help from the law. From what I've heard there isn't any north of the border. And the farther up we go, the worse it gets. And Skagway's only about twenty feet from the pole."

At the head of the Lynn Canal, the terminus of Alaska's inland passage, twin fjordlike valleys lie between the rugged, seven-thousand-foot-high mountains. Dyea occupies one valley, Skagway, home of the north wind and the beginning of the White Pass route to the headwaters of the Yukon, the other. Skagway, threshold of the wilderness, scooped out of the mountains, with its brawling glacial stream dashing through the dark spruce forests to join the clear, blue waters of the Lynn Canal.

A bell had sounded interrupting Perry's and Horne's conversation. A voice announced Skagway; they went out on deck. There lay their destination directly ahead, the last port of call on the Inside Passage, a sprawl of houses, hotels, stores, false-front buildings, banks, saloons, dance halls, and gambling houses facing one another across dirt streets. The harbor was crowded with vessels of all sizes. The rickity dock was piled with cargo. The *Charles E. Sterling* dropped anchor about a mile from it. A ferry rode the high tide out to meet her and relieve her of her passengers.

Perry took one look at the town and gasped. "Great Caesar's ghost, it's the end of the world!"

"End of the run," said Captain Bairsford behind them. "All the ships turn around here. No point in going farther, up the Skagway River. How long ye boys plan on staying?"

"Not long," murmured Perry. "If it were up to me, we'd be starting back this afternoon."

"We'll be," said the captain. "If ye' decide to come, we'll be leaving at three sharp."

"We're here for a while," said Horne. "Where's the best place to stay?"

"The Golden North Hotel. When ye land, head up Broadway Street. It's at Third and Broadway. Look for the golden dome."

Carrying hand luggage only, they were among the first to board the ferry. Within ten minutes it was on its way to the dock, the *Charles E. Sterling* slipping behind them.

Perry gazed at it longingly. "I have a sneaky feeling I'm making a big mistake, leaving that tub," he muttered.

"Nonsense. Why so fidgety all of a sudden?"

"Nothing sudden about it. I know more than I care to know about this hellhole. It's the last frontier in spades. It makes Deadwood look like a monastery garden."

"Will you relax? Look at the scenery, it's magnificent."

Instead, Perry cast a last wistful look at the *Charles E. Sterling.*

The ferry dock was piled with crates, boxes, and large drums, leaving scarcely room for the new arrivals to thread their way through to dry land and Broadway Street. Perry and Horne found themselves near the head of the parade. They rounded a stack of oil drums, coming within sight of the street when a shot rang out. A flurry of firing followed and in an instant the air was filled with lead coming from opposite ends of the dock. Men bellowed and cursed and dropped. Horne ducked, pulling Perry down with him, but not quickly enough. A shot ripped through Perry's right sleeve near the cuff. He stared at it for a second as if he couldn't believe it had happened. The shooting became heavier, the air quickly filling with smoke. Someone, for some inexplicable reason, targeted Perry. He dove behind a barrel, landing heavily but unhurt; but his momentum carried him to the edge of the dock and off it into the water. He came up sputtering and livid, cursing vehemently. Horne reached out to help him back up onto the dock. Perry waved him away and sat back down, his head barely above the surface of the water, one cheek flattened against the beam supporting the cross-planking.

"It's safer down here, damnit!"

The supplies piled about obstructed their view of the participants. All either of them could do was crouch— Perry in the water, Horne on the dock—cover their heads, and wait out the hostilities, fuming. Presently the shooting stopped. All was quiet for a long moment. Horne helped Perry out of the water. He was soaked to the skin and shivering; mud caked his shoes and trousers all the way up to his knees. Horne tried to help him wring out his clothing, but he pushed away angrily.

"Leave me alone! You and your damned wild-goose chases! Just get me to the damned hotel, though if I was twenty years younger, I'd swim back to the goddamned ship and get the hell out of here!"

The room assigned to them in the Golden North Hotel was spacious, comfortable, and expensive: twenty dollars a night. Horne ordered up a plunge bath for Perry, and while he was relaxing in the tub and chasing the chill from his bones, Horne went out and got him a bottle of an excellent Armagnac brandy. It helped to calm the troubled waters, but Perry persisted in his negative view of the town. He put on his other suit and draped the jacket and trousers of his soaked one over the backs of chairs to dry.

Horne insisted that he relax for a while, rest up from

his ordeal, and enjoy his brandy before venturing forth in search of DeBlois.

"No, thank you. The quicker I get at it, the sooner my part is over with." He donned his still-somewhat-soggy flap-brimmed hat, scowled reproachfully, and started for the door. He paused with his hand on the nob. "Let me have your forty-five."

"Are you serious?"

"Do I sound like I'm joking?"

"You've never worn a gun in your life. You hate guns."

"With a passion. Hand it over."

"Perry . . ."

"Give it here! A soldier doesn't go into the fighting without firearms; you can't expect me to waltz around without protection. This isn't a town—it's a battlefield!"

He strode over to Horne, unbuckled his belt, and whipped it off, holster, gun, and all.

"I wish you wouldn't—"

"Nephew, if I have to do your dirty work for you, the least you can do is let me do it my way. Is the damn thing loaded?"

"Always. Be careful. Good Lord, I'll bet you can't hit the side of a barn. Whatever you do, don't shoot yourself in the foot."

Perry snorted, glowered, and left, slamming the door. The instant he was gone, second thoughts began assailing Horne. It was a mistake, he never should have let him carry the thing; still, Perry wouldn't have left without it, and he did have good reason to be fearful.

The streets outside sounded like Deadwood hosting a convention of high-line riders. Not a minute passed without a gun going off. Captain Bairsford had mentioned that the law in Skagway was represented by a single deputy marshal. With so much gold and profits from the diggings floating about town, it was no wonder bad blood was continually on the boil. Cheechakos—tender foots—from the States and sourdoughs, drifting down out of the mountains, trudged about the streets, tripling the permanent population. Skagway itself—that is the land upon which it stood—had reputedly been stolen from the homestead of one Ben Moore, the first settler in the area; without regard for laws or property rights, gold-seekers, adventurers, and ruffians invaded the area, took what they wanted, set up tents, built the docks, laid out the streets, sold lots, and established businesses. Such a melee of disorder and confusion could not help but invite unscrupulous speculators, confidence men, and scoundrels. Crooks took advantage of unwary new arrivals, fleecing them of their stake money, injuring, even murdering them.

The business community carried on a cutthroat war with Dyea, Valdez, St. Michael, Edmonton, and the Stikine route for preeminence as the gateway to the Klondike with the profits to be made from the traffic flowing in and out of Dawson. But Skagway was not all violence and disorder. It was a town with opportunities for anyone rugged and patient enough to seize the bit.

Perry, unfortunately, was the furthest thing from such enterprising types. He was in his seventies and had slowed considerably in the past two years. He'd left the hotel in a foul mood, not quite as foul as when they arrived there an hour earlier, but foul enough. He was not a man to resist speaking his mind; his tongue could be a two-edged sword when his dander was up. If he happened to cross the wrong individual out there, even though he was armed, he'd be at grave risk. Were he not carrying a gun, he'd be less so, but when he left he was in no mood to defer to this wisdom.

"Dear Lord, please bring him back safe and sound . . ."

Horne poured himself a brandy downed it in one swig, and sat on the edge of the bed to await his return. He listened worriedly to the sporadic gunfire, the shouting and screaming, drifting up from the street below.

One hand on his gun, the other holding his hat on against a lively breeze blowing from the mountains, Perry began wondering about Skagway. After about twenty minutes of exploring he was able to measure the town as four blocks wide by fourteen long. The Skagway River wandered northward along the west side. To the east the forest marched up close to town and through the trees ran the Dewey Lakes Trail. He was walking along Ninth Avenue in the center of town, sidestepping one group of boisterous drunken sourdoughs after another, when he stopped short and, turning, looked upward.

"Well, well, well, up jumped the devil. What do you know about that?"

It was a store, a very large store with a long black and gold sign separating the ground and second floors:

L DeBLOIS, LTD.
FINE FURS BOUGHT & SOLD

The windows wore iron grates over them; protection against the carousing rabble, he decided. In the windows hung a variety of pelts: silver fox, white fox, blue fox, fisher, mink, musk-ox, muskrat, raccoon, sable, brown and black wolf, gray wolf.

The door rang a bell when Perry opened it. There was a long counter fronting space for an office. Filing cabinets stood against the back wall and a large safe. Whoever the manufacturer was, time had obliterated his name on the door. There was a spacious flattop desk. On either side, of the office area, stretching approximately thirty feet, were racks with pelts hanging from them. In the rear alongside the safe, stairs ascended to the second floor.

The man behind the counter was in his shirtsleeves. He appeared to be the only one in the place. From Horne's description he could only be Lucien DeBlois. One small detail confirmed it. Centering the front of his shirt was Horne's diamond horseshoe stickpin.

"May I help you, *monsieur?*"

Horne had nearly finished the bottle. As time went on he was becoming increasingly nervous and worried over Perry. Twice he nearly put on his jacket to go out looking for him, only to think better of it. He should be returning shortly.

He stopped pacing and stood looking down into the street. It was dirt that in the spring rains must turn into an impassable quagmire. From what he could see of the buildings opposite up and down the street, the Golden North Hotel was a pearl among the swine: newer, better, more solidly built, an expensive piece of construction among the jerry-built and cheap prefabricated structures surrounding it.

He poured another drink. What time was it? he wondered. Late afternoon, getting on toward five. It wouldn't start to get dark for another hour, even this far north.

"Perry, Perry . . ."

"Armitage is the name: Henry Wadsworth Longfellow Armitage. From New York City. I have the honor to represent a syndicate of furriers: Halberstam, the DeGroat Brothers, Finlay's, all the biggest and most successful dealers."

"Delighted to meet you, sir. And what may I do for you?"

"I heard about you down in Juneau. Your reputation is such I simply had to come up and see you."

"How flattering . . ."

"I'll get right to the point. The people I represent have been having a hard time finding a quality source of supply. The past few months the product that's been coming in has been poor quality.. Mediocre pelts; old, dried out, perfectly fine pelts damaged: trap teeth marks, pelts hastily and carelessly removed. What we're looking for is a reliable source of supply."

"You have come to zee right place."

"That's what they told me down in Juneau."

"Permeet me to show you some specimens. Note, I do not *say* my finest specimens; all are top-grade. I deal weeth only zee best and most reliable trappers. Here, a seelver fox. Feel eet." He produced a magnifying glass from a desk drawer. "Examine eet closely. Notice how close and fine zee underwool ees. I don't have to tell you zat zee fur upon zee necks usually runs dark, as black as zis one. I happen to have a number of pelts with zee fur black halfway, even three-quarters of zere length. Natural black foxes, enormously expensive. But for you I am sure we can, ah, deescuss zee price."

"Beautiful."

"No markeengs, no trap teeth marks, no damage of any sort. Look closely, please. Good professional trappers, men who pride zemselves on zere technique and equipment, use only zee Newhouse trap. You are familiar weeth zee Newhouse trap?"

"I've heard of it. I've never seen one."

"Let me show you."

He brought out a six-inch jaw, double-spring otter trap and demonstrated how it worked, continuing to laud the Newhouse trap as the finest ever made.

"My suppliers have supplied me for years. And excluseevely. Only top professionals qualify to supply DeBlois. Ask anyone. I have a written contract weeth every trapper. Let me show you."

Please do, thought Perry. I'd like nothing better than a peek inside your safe. There's sure to be a strongbox, sure to be money in it. Sixty thousand and forty dollars? Hopefully, T.G. This is incredible. To walk into this place cold and spot his stickpin. Wait till I tell him. Where is the thieving scum keeping his Jürgensen?

DeBlois had unlocked and opened the safe. Perry craned his neck left and right trying to look around him into the safe, but before the Frenchman arose from his stoop and moved out of the line of sight, he closed the door almost all the way. He brought over a thick sheaf of contracts.

"I drew up zee agreement myself. Eet's very simple. Eet states zee goeeng rate for every type of pelt, steepulates zat zee pelt must be een excellent condition, eendicates zat zee supplier shall receive his payment promptly, and een cash and zee expeeration date ees een zee lower left-hand corner."

"A very good system. Are you by chance also a lawyer?"

"*Mais non* You flatter me."

"It certainly protects you both."

"I can get you anything. Even Kodiak bear. Black, brown greezly, whatever your heart desires."

"Whatever milady's heart desires," said Perry. "The grandes dames of New York City have husbands who are rolling in money; they can afford the very best available. However, I must caution you, I shall be looking for quite large quantities."

"No order can be too large to feel, I assure you . . ."

"That's good to hear. How do you ship?"

"By boat down to Seattle and by rail throughout zee States. Now, as to price—"

"Excuse me, but I think we can postpone discussing the details."

"You are goeeng?"

"I'll be back. I must send a telegram to my people and tell them their problem appears to be solved."

"Tell zem you have found zee pot of gold at zee rainbow's end, an endless supply of zee finest furs een North America."

"Excellent, excellent. Until tomorrow morning, then. By the way, how late are you open?"

"Unteel seex o'clock. Open at eight o'clock tomorrow morneeng."

"Excellent. I shall be back bright and early."

He was staring at Horne's stickpin.

DeBlois noticed. "Ees eet not beautiful? I won eet een a poker game."

"Lucky fellow."

Clapping his hat on, Perry hurried out; once outside, he got his bearings and set out for the hotel.

8

It was almost five o'clock by the time Perry got back to the room. Horne greeted him irritably, unbuckling his belt and whipping it off.

"Where've you been? I've been worried sick." He buckled on his gun

"What for? I can take care of myself, even in this Gemorrah. Don't you want to know what happened?"

Horne's eyes brightened as Perry detailed the highlights of his meeting with DeBlois.

"Best of all, he's there alone. Right now. Will be until six. You can go over and beard the lion in his den. On second thought, you wouldn't be so rash . . ."

"Try me. Why pass up a golden opportunity? You say you couldn't see inside the safe?"

"No, but I'm sure he keeps cash in it. He must. The trappers come in with their pelts, he pays them in cash. It's in the contract he showed me. But, really, you think it's wise to go barging in?"

"You did."

"Not to put a gun to his head and demand sixty thousand dollars."

"Minor distinction. There was no sign of my watch."

"He's got your pin, I can't imagine he'd unload the watch. It's rather a prize with that diamond embedded in the stem."

"I'm going."

"Wait, wait. What's your hurry? It's only six blocks up the street. You still have almost an hour before he closes. If you have to burst in on him, at least wait until near closing time. That way there won't be anybody to interrupt you."

"You're right."

"When am I not? T.G. . . ."

"Mmmm."

"Listen to me, and please don't cut me off. If anything happens, if somebody does blunder in and make a mess of things, if he forces you to shoot, anything to prevent your getting out of there clean, you mustn't forget one thing. There's only the two of you involved. His hitting you on the head comes down to your word against his. And you admitted you never saw him."

"I smelled him. Orange blossoms. Did he smell of orange blossoms in the store?"

"I didn't notice. The point I'm trying to make is if the thing winds up in court, you'll have one hell of a time proving your case."

"I have no intention of letting it get that far."

"You may not, but you don't have absolute control either."

"The man's a skulking coward. One look at this"—he patted his gun—"he'll wilt. He'll give me the sky."

"I wish I had your optimism. Don't you think you ought to plan an escape route just in case? Where you'll run to if you have to?"

"Back here."

"That's great. And he'll follow you, and no doubt pick up the deputy marshal on the way, and accuse you of robbing him. What will you say to that? He robbed me first? What I'm trying to say is it's not as cut-and-dried as you obviously want it to be. On the contrary, it's a sack of snakes. A mess. If you have to make a run for it, where will you go? Into the woods? Up onto the glacier? To the gold fields? Face facts, you're stuck here. You've caught up with him, but you haven't got him, he's got you. You hit him up for your money, he'll probably laugh in your face. I would."

"We'll see. I've come this far . . ."

"All the more reason to take extra special care from now on. Do whatever you do right."

"You have a suggestion?"

"Not a one. It's your chestnuts in the fire. I've done my job. I can hang around and give you moral support, but don't expect me to testify in your behalf. I wasn't in the room when you claim he clobbered you."

"What the hell are you talking about 'claim'?"

"Wrong word, sorry. Nevertheless, you don't have a witness. He knows that. He knows he's got you over a barrel. Look, I'll come with you. I can at least stand outside and make sure nobody walks in on you. But frankly, I can only see one way for you to get your valuables back and your money and not have him chasing after you."

"Shoot him."

"Exactly."

Perry continued talking like a Dutch uncle to him all the way down to the lobby and out the door. They stood on the board sidewalk before the entrance. Horne took a deep breath and let it out slowly. Single-minded obstinacy had taken firm hold of his conviction, but Perry persisted in pointing out all the possible repercussions.

"Think about it. If you confront him and he doesn't come across, the bottom'll drop out of the whole business. You will have tipped your hand, lost the one thing in your favor: the element of surprise. He could even have you arrested for threatening him with a gun. He's probably the best of friends with the deputy marshal. They could be lodge brothers . . ."

"Lay off, will you? You can come along, just put a lid on it."

"This is lunacy. But why am I surprised? It's happened before with you; held up and robbed in a game. More than once, as I recall. Only you've always had witnesses and you were able to retaliate right away. Not like this. T.G., promise me you won't do anything violent. It can only backfire on you."

Shooting erupted close by. Horne swore and ducked instinctively. Perry was a split second late lowering his head. A slug passed cleaning through his hat, parting his hair. The color drained from his face; his eyes swam with fear. He staggered slightly and backed into the protection of the hotel entrance. His knees were knocking, his lower lip quivered as he took off his hat and poked his finger through each hole in turn.

"G-g-g-great C-c-c-caesar's g-g-g-ghost. That does it!"

Color game surging back into his cheeks. He exploded. He dashed his hat to the sidewalk and kicked it into the street.

"I'm leaving this hell hole. Right now!"

"Calm down, it was a fluke, a stray shot—"

"That came within half an inch of blowing my brains out. I'm gone. I'm going up, packing, getting down to that accursed dock, and putting myself on the first tub out. If there isn't one, I'll buy one. If I can't buy one, I'll steal one."

"You'd walk about on me, desert me?"

"I did my bit. There's nothing more I can do. I'll be damned if I'll stay in this godforsaken dung heap two minutes more than have to."

On he raved, but through his tirade, his eloquent and colorful condemnation of Skagway and its residential rubble came the clear, unmistakable voice of fear. His eyes were suffused with it. His voice cracked with it. His knees knocked, lip quivered, and he could not keep his hands still. He was terrified of being murdered, gunned down by someone he wouldn't even see in a place he thoroughly despised.

"I never should have come to in the first place. Why I listen to you . . ."

"Where will you go?"

"Back to San Antonio. New Orleans. Kansas City. Anyplace where ruffians and scalawags, scoundrels and scum don't walk around shooting at one another and at innocent bystanders. Great God, we hadn't even set foot on dry land before they began blasting. We were lucky to get off that dock alive. If you've half a brain in that stubborn skull of yours, you'll drop this idiotic vendetta and come with me."

"I have unfinished business."

"Fine. Go to it. Good luck!" Into the hotel he stormed.

Horne sighed, shrugged, shook his head, and started off up the street. He covered the six blocks and turned the corner into Ninth Avenue. He approached the store, paused before the door to look up and down the street, and walked in. DeBlois was sitting at his desk reading a newspaper. Horne turned and bolted the door, then began to pull down the windowshades.

DeBlois got up and came to the counter. "What zee devil . . . What do you sink you are doeeng?"

His expression was that of puzzled curiosity. Horne failed to see the slightest glint of recognition in his eyes.

"Beautiful, Lucien. Cool as a cucumber."

"I beg your pardon. Have we met?"

Horne pulled down the last shade. "Let's not start off playing games okay? They bore me. I'll make it short." He reached across the counter and snatched away his stickpin. "Give me my watch and my sixty thousand."

"What do you theenk you are doeeng? Geev me back my peen theese eenstant!"

"Keep it up." Horne scowled and drew his .45. "My watch and money. Move!" DeBlois gaped and started to raise his hands. "Keep your hands down. Open the safe."

"You are makeeng a 'orrible mistake, *monsieur*. You have zee wrong man. Take zee steeckpeen and go, please. Get out, leave me een peace."

"Listen to me, Lucien . . ."

"Ah hah, zat ees your mistake. Zat ees zee second time you have call me zat. My name ees not Lucien, eet ees Louis."

"Sure, and Lucien is your twin brother."

"Zat ees so."

"You're beautiful. You never quit. I'll give you ten seconds to open that safe and give me my money or so help me God I'll blow your head off."

"*Monsieur*, you are being very foolish. I am telleeng you zee truth. Lucien *ees* my brother, alas. To my regret. Such a burden. I have always say one day he weel be zee death of me."

"Today's the day if you don't get a move on."

"Please leesten, I beg you. Eef you had trouble eet was weeth Lucien, not me. I am decent and law-abideeng. I do not lie, I am no thief. Whatever was done to you I did not do eet. He stole from you seexty thousand dollars? I believe you; he ees capable of eet. I do not have such a sum on hand. Only a few hundred. I can geeve you zat . . ."

Horne stared at him for a long time without speaking. DeBlois stared back and swallowed repeatedly. Horne waved the gun.

"You lie through your goddamn teeth. You're no more twins than I am. Oh, you can call yourself by two names, claim two identities. But you're him; you look like him, sound like him, act like him. And this cinches it." He held up the stickpin. "He stole it from me. So what are you doing with it?"

"He gave eet to me. I swear!"

"Of course."

"Eet ees zee truth! He did not tell me where he got eet. I presumed he took eet een payment for a debt. He does not tell me how he leaves, what he does. I do not ask. I do not want to know. Eef you were saddled weeth a brother, a black sheep, would you want to know what he was· up to? Dear God een heaven, you cannot believe zee agonies zat man has put me through."

"Just shut up, you're beginning to bore. Get busy and open the safe."

"Yes, yes."

Still holding the gun on him, Horne lifted the hinged

counter board and joined him inside. DeBlois knelt,
fiddled with the combination, and pulled open the door.
The safe was crammed with envelopes, papers, stock
certificates. There was also a gun. On the bottom shelf
was a large, square strongbox.

"Give me the gun. Grip first."

DeBlois obeyed. Horne shoved it in his belt.

"Get out the box and open it."

DeBlois did so. Using a key suspended from a silver
chain around his neck, he opened it. It was filled with
bills in large denominations.

"Only a few hundred, isn't that what you said?"

"Take eet, take eet all!"

"Don't be so generous, all I want is what's coming to
me. Start counting out loud. Sixty thousand and forty
dollars."

"Yes, yes."

Horne got down on his knees to get a better look
inside the safe. Something glinted at the rear of the
second shelf. He ducked lower and peered in.

"My watch!" he uttered in triumphant.

Uttered and a sledgehammer struck, slamming him
in the side of the head, caving it in, sending crimson
flashes through his brain. Over he fell. The last thing
he saw was a host of pelts in close formation above him.
Luxurious. Beautiful. His skull exploded. Out he went.

9

Perry arrived at the dock hatless, bag in hand, still fuming, outraged by his brush with death. He stormed up to an old man sitting on a piling whittling. His little eyes under his fisherman's cap looked up from his work and questioningly at Perry.

"When's the next boat out of this hole?"

The man turned and indicated. *"Ocean Queen."*

A paddle wheeler sat at anchor a mile out. Men swarmed about the deck. The ferry was approaching, carrying passengers and their luggage and freight; it was heading for the dock about twenty yards from where Perry stood.

"When it leaving?"

"Search me. Soon, I 'magine. Ships gen'ally come in, discharge passengers, take 'em on, and turn 'round and leave. Don' gen'ally stay ovahnight. Not gen'ally."

"Where's it bound for?"

"Seattle, Portlan', dunno. Say, be you mad at somethin'?"

"Skagway! Can I ask you a personal question? How can you live in such a sinkhole. This place is Sodom and Gomorrah wrapped into one. All people do is shoot at one another and hit everybody else. Raise hell, carry on like lunatics."

"I like it. It's purty."

"It's Dante's inferno with scenery. Satan himself would be afraid to live here. Anybody with an ounce of sense would. Good day and good luck! I hope nobody plugs you on the way home."

Perry stomped off toward the ferry landing. He had covered about ten yards when a man popped up from behind a crate, scaring the living daylights out of him. He stifled a scream. The man, bearded, filthy, ragged, and stinking of stale liquor, jammed a gun at his midsection.

"Hol' it right there, Pop, lessee the inside o' your wallet."

Perry's anger had not appreciably subsided since the errant slug found the crown of his hat. He did manage to bridle his ire long enough to address the whittler civilly, but when he left him, it resurfaced. He seethed, muttering to himself, reviling Skagway. The holdup man's abrupt intrusion, popping up like a jack-in-the-box as he had, frightening him within an inch of heart seizure, infuriated him.

His response to the demand was a low growling that speedily developed into a maniacal roar. He hauled off and smashed the bum full in the face, knocking him off the dock into the drink. He landed on his back and began floundering and bellowing, splashing water in every direction.

"I can't swim! Help me! Help me!"

His strenuous exertions brought him closer to the dock. He looked upward, a pleading expression on his ugly face, sputtering, spitting water, splashing loudly.

"I can't swim!"

Perry set one foot against his face and pushed him under.

"Then drown, you miscreant son of a bitch!"

Perry purchased passage to Portland and was settling into his cabin, which was palatial compared to the one he and Horne had shared on the way up. After he unpacked he went out on deck for a last look at Skagway.

His anger, frustration, and fear having abated to some degree, his conscience began to trouble him. T.G. was right: he *was* deserting his nephew. He should hang around if only to provide moral support. But he simply could not. Skagway frightened him more than any town he'd ever been in, and he'd been in many a hell hole. But Skagway seemed to pinpoint him as its prime target: isolating him, fixing on him, and determined to destroy him. There was another aspect to the thing: the place was so remote, ultima Thule, the end of the world, sitting in the shadow of the glacier, separated from civilization by a thousand dreary miles.

"Never again."

He set his hand over his heart. It was beating normally for the first time in an hour. Actually for the first time since they'd set foot on the inbound ferry. The fracas on the dock had upset him; the continuous gunfire in town kept fear at the forefront of his mind and quickened his heartbeat. The shot through his hat had nearly stopped it, a had the jack-in-the-box.

He wondered how Horne was faring, but could not begin to guess. He did hope that T.G. would not lose his temper and substitute his .45 for his common sense. Still, he was incapable of shooting anybody in cold blood, even one who had wronged him as callously as had the Frenchman. From the little he had seen of DeBlois, he didn't appear up to such a heinous crime, but of course it was impossible to judge such a thing. With a little luck Horne would get something back for his trouble, if not the entire amount at least a part, hopefully something . . .

"And get out of that miserable place alive."

He could understand T.G.'s wanting to catch up with DeBlois and square things between them. Were Perry thirty years younger and wronged in such a manner, he would do the same—only with better preparation and some thought as to how to get out without spilling blood, his own or the other fellow's. He'd give Horne two weeks. By then he himself would be back down in Texas. Horne could contact him in San Antonio if he was interested. San Antonio or Kansas City or New

Orleans. They always stayed at the same hotel in every town. They'd been separated before many times and always managed to get back together. And when they met again, Skagway and its dangers and lawlessness would be well behind them and not fit subject for pleasant dinner conversation.

"Take care of yourself, my boy. Do what you must and get out of there as fast as you can."

Leaving Skagway was the furthest thing from Horne's mind when he regained consciousness. His most immediate concern was his health—in particular the condition of his head. He sat in a cramped, evil-smelling and dank cell on the edge of a narrow cot that was chained to the wall. Someone had bandaged his head. Why they'd bothered he had no idea. It certainly didn't alleviate the throbbing pain or dispel the bright flashes issuing from his beleaguered brain, shooting outward and dissolving against the wall of his skull. It was fractured, no question. It had to be. Concussion wasn't nearly so painful.

A man was standing outside his cell door. He was tall, ungainly, with a friendly crooked smile. He was perhaps thirty, but already losing his hair in the front. He combed it down over his forehead to conceal its departure. A badge was pinned to his plaid shirt pocket.

"How we doing?"

"I have a fractured skull," Horne said as loudly as was necessary to be heard, for each syllable triggered a small needle in the area of the fracture just above his temple.

"No you don't. I checked when I bandaged you."

"It's fractured."

"Concussion. You're getting a nice lump there, but there was no sign of blood or any other fluid from your mouth or nose or ears. You haven't vomited. You obviously don't have any speech difficulty. You're not sleepy. No double vision, have you?"

"You a doctor?"

"I might as well be. I patch up more prisoners than any two doctors. I'm John Meriweather, Deputy Marshal."

"What am I doing here?"

"Can't you guess? You're under arrest. Mr. DeBlois signed the complaint. A laundry list of charge: attempted robbery, threatening bodily harm, threatening to blow his head off, extortion . . ."

"Mr. DeBlois has everything turned inside out."

"Tell me about it."

"Would it make any difference?"

"It could."

Hurdlesford, $60,040, diamond horseshoe stickpin, watch, robbery, and a long pursuit to Skagway. Deputy Marshal Meriweather listened politely but, when Horne was done, made no comment.

"You're not saying anything," said Horne. "I guess it doesn't make any difference."

"I'm thinking. You keep saying Lucien DeBlois."

"That's what he called himself."

"That's his name. Your mistake was you were dealing with his brother Louis."

"Oh, my God . . ."

Meriweather nodded. "Identical twins—identical in looks, but definitely not in character. Lucien is a renegade, always has been. Louis is a pillar of the community, one of the few. I doubt if there's a more highly respected businessman in the whole area. Didn't Louis tell you he was Louis?"

Horne nodded slowly and cautiously.

"Then why didn't you believe him?" Meriweather asked.

"Under the circumstances, would you?"

The deputy marshal considered this for a moment. "Probably not."

"He slammed me in the head with a safe door. I wasn't paying attention. I spotted my watch inside the safe and bent over for a closer look."

"Tough luck."

"Can I see a doctor?"

"Still hurts bad, eh?"

"It's fractured."

"It's not, but I'll send somebody over to Doc Shaker's; he'll come have a look. Maybe he can give you a pill to ease the pain."

"He a real doctor?"

"I can't say. He says he is and he's been doctoring Skagway for three years with no complaints I've ever heard about."

"What happens to me now?"

"One of two things. Either Louis'll have second thoughts, take pity on you, and drop the charges. Or we take you down to Juneau to stand trial."

"I'd like that."

Meriweather jerked his head back like a chicken on the strut. "You would?"

"I'd like to get him into court. Hear him answer a few questions. I'll sue the son of a bitch."

"On what grounds?"

"Possession of stolen merchandise for starters. That was my watch in his safe." He paused and searched his pockets. "He had my stickpin. Where the hell—"

"What?"

"He must have taken it back when he clobbered me."

"Can you prove the watch is yours?"

"My initials are on the back: T.G.H."

"T . . ."

"My name is T.G. Horne. You get hold of that watch and check the back, you'll see."

"I prefer not to get involved. That part of it's not my job. It's evidence. It'll be presented in court if you want it to be. Along with the pin. All I'm supposed to do is arrest the culprit. He filed the complaint, here you are."

"Let me tell you something, and it's not my head, I'm not crazy: he told me he was Louis, only I didn't believe him. Not then, not now. Oh, they're twins all right, I'll give you that, only he's Lucien, not Louis."

"Mister, you're blowing smoke. Must be your head."

"Will you listen? If he was Louis, what was he doing with my watch and stickpin? If Lucien did come back here, which I'm sure he did—he does come to Skagway, doesn't he?"

Meriweather nodded. "Now and then."

"He came back with my money, my valuables. Now you tell me, why in the name of common sense would he hand over an eight-hundred-dollar diamond pin and a thousand-dollar Jürgensen watch to Louis? Why? Does he owe him?"

"I wouldn't know. Why didn't you ask him?"

"Why bother? He wasn't giving me answers, he was talking in circles, mostly whining about Lucien. But I'm convinced, and nobody can tell me otherwise, the one in the store was Lucien."

"Impossible. Besides, it doesn't make sense."

"Looking into his eyes as we talked, his mannerisms, everything about him—I mean down to the tiniest detail he was Lucien."

"Did he smell like he smelled when he conked you over the head back in Kansas?"

"No . . ."

"Then not everything was Lucien."

"Everything else, goddammit!"

"Don't be upset with me, I'm neutral. I'm trying to help. You got a bad concussion."

"Fracture."

"Have it your way. Man, are you always this stubborn? Anyway, you shouldn't overdo it. Why don't you lie down until the doc gets here? After, I'll bring you something to eat. Lie down." He started off.

"Wait, one more question. When Lucien comes to Skagway does he stay with Louis?"

" 'Far as I know."

"So he could be here now. It could have been him I

talked to; it's not impossible. One other thing: which one is married to Marion?"

Meriweather's eyes widened. "Louis. How do you know about her?"

"Horne told him. "The little I got to know the lady I got the impression she doesn't have a very high regard for her husband."

"And how do you know that?"

"Intuition."

"You're right. They've been on the verge of splitting up for a couple years. They say around town she's got a thing for Lucien. 'They' say. Still, there could be some truth to it. Louis is pretty stuffy, straitlaced, boring. Lucien's much more exciting, even if he does trail a long shadow. You know the type of men that attract some women. I'll go and get the doc."

After Meriweather left, Horne lay back on his cot. Down the narrow, dimly lit hallway he could hear the occupants of the holding pen: boisterous carrying on, drunken singing, laughter. They'd be let out in the morning. He'd be here and the following day on his way to Juneau to be locked up to await trial. But if he looked at the dark side, what could they do to him if he was convicted? Give him at least a year. Where? Where was the penitentiary in Alaska? Juneau, Nome, Anchorage? More important, how bad was it?

He closed his eyes and tried to sleep.

" 'Ello again, *monsieur*."

It was Lucien. Or Louis. One or the other, wearing his stickpin and watch, the chain slung across his vest.

"Beat it!"

"Please, do not be eenhospitable. I just dropped een to tell you no hard feelings."

Horne sat up. Bringing his head up with him detonated violent pain. It felt as if his brain had rolled over completely inside his skull. He groaned and rubbed his temples lightly.

"Does that mean you'll drop the charges?"

"Oh, *mais non*, I could do zat. After what you deed?"

"So what did you come for, to rub salt in the wound? Go away."

"I am goeeng. I can see you are een severe pain; eet ees a heavy door. Rest, you weel feel better. Just one other theeng: you were right." He nodded, leering, and lowered his voice. "I am Lucien."

"Don't bother admitting it. I know."

"Ah, but now you have eet, as zey say, from zee horse's mouth, *nez-pas?* Ha, for all zee good eet weel do you. No one weel believe you eef you tell zem, least of all John Meriweather. *Bon soir, mon ami.* See you een court."

10

Doc Shaker had a face that looked as if it had been molded out of bread dough, then baked to a shiny light brown. He was starting a beard; it was in the scraffy stage and looked ridiculous. His clothes smelled of mothballs and he kept his fedora on all the while he ministered to the patient. Deputy Marshal Meriweather stood outside the cell looking on.

"It's fractured," muttered Horne.

"Only concussion." He finished applying a fresh bandage to Horne's suffering head. "I'm gonna give ya a box o' Hammond's Six-eighty. Homeopathic pain pills. Take two every four hours, stay calm, and eat lots o' soup." He dug the box of pills out of his bag, restored his stethoscope and what remained of the roll of gauze, and snapped the bag shut. "That'll be a buck anna half."

Horne fished out his wallet. It felt suspiciously light. It was empty.

"Jesus Christ! I had over seventeen hundred bucks. It's gone, every cent! The son of a bitch stole it."

"You sayin' you're broke?" Doc Shaker was eyeing him worriedly.

"I'll take care of it," said Meriweather, and paid him.

"Thanks," Horne said. "I'll reimburse you."

"Sure."

Shaker left.

"Cheer up," said Meriweather. "I got some beef and

barley soup, succotash, fresh-baked biscuits, and good coffee. You get something in you you'll feel a hundred percent better."

"I was lying on the floor out cold and he picked my pocket. Incredible! He never stops."

"Are you sure you had the money with you when you went in?"

"Of course! I wouldn't leave it in the hotel room."

"Just asking." Meriweather scratched his forehead through his thinning hair and frowned. "That's funny."

"Hilarious."

"No, I mean for Louis to rob you. He's no thief. Lucien, on the other hand . . ."

"I keep telling you it *was* Lucien. He admitted it outright when he stopped by before, and said if I told anybody he'd deny it. Let me ask you something, putting my claim of one substituting for the other aside for the moment, have you seen the two of them at the same time around town lately?"

"Not that I recall . . ."

"I wonder if anybody has?"

"What are you getting at?"

"I wonder if Louis is still around, still alive."

"Why wouldn't he be?"

"You said before he and Marion were on the outs; she has a thing for his brother. How serious is it? Serious enough that they'd want him out of the picture?"

Meriweather snickered. "You're blowing smoke again. They don't have to kill Louis to get rid of him. Don't have to get rid of him, period. They could just run off together."

"I wonder where she is." He told him about Captain Bairsford dropping here and Mr. K. off at Cape Saint James on the way up. "I wonder if when they were picked up by another ship they continued on their way up here or headed back?"

"I haven't seen her around town. You now, it strikes me you'd be doing yourself a favor if you dropped all this speculating, letting your imagination run away with you. It's only upsetting you; you heard the doc, he told you to stay calm."

"It's not upsetting me in the least. If I can put all the pieces together properly I might be able to turn the whole thing to my advantage. What have I got to lose trying? By the way, if—and I do mean if—worse comes to worst and I'm convicted, how long can they give me?"

"I couldn't begin to guess: attempted grand larceny, attempted murder."

"Murder my foot!"

"You did threaten to kill him."

"They can't hang me."

"Of course not. They'll sentence you to prison. You'll go to Sitka, the territorial capital."

"Is the prison . . ."

"Bad? Rough? From what I hear it's not exactly a picnic. Remember, we're only a territory, so we don't get much money from the federal government. Everything, including the prison facilities, is a little on the primitive side."

"So I've noticed."

"But aren't you putting the cart before the horse? You haven't even gone to trial yet. You may not; Louis might change his mind and drop the charges."

"Louis might; Lucien never will."

Horne felt better the next day, which surprised him. The pain in his head reduced itself to a dull, bearable aching. Meriweather escorted him down to Juneau aboard the daily steam packet. He had the decency to put him on his honor and not shackle him for public display. T.G. had come to like the man and appreciated his kindnesses. He was the only law in Skagway and could have been a petty tyrant, using his badge as a license to brutalize his prisoners and otherwise make life miserable for them. Others did, alibiing their viciousness, claiming it discouraged potential lawbreakers. But Meriweather treated everyone humanely, with patience and dignity, even the hardest cases, the serious menaces to the community who might better have been shot on sight.

The deputy marshall delivered him to the jail and into the custody of Marshal Henry "Hank" Sinatra, who had to be close to seventy, was cool, evidently capable, and appeared bored by the whole business: accepting another prisoner, assigning him to a cell, diving into the necessary paperwork. He wasn't unfriendly; he did not hard-eye him accusingly when Meriweather introduced them or question why he wasn't in irons. He simply didn't seem interested; he also seemed incapable of smiling, displaying or emitting human warmth that one could so readily associate with the deputy marshal. Horne was locked in and Sinatra left the two of them in privacy.

"I want to thank you for everything, John," said Horne as he shook his hand through the bars. "You've been very decent, very helpful. I appreciate it."

"Good luck, T.G. I shouldn't say it, but this whole mess does feel like you're getting a raw deal, especially his stealing your money from your wallet. I'm back and forth two or three times a week. I'll probably be here when you go on trial. If you want I'd be willing to testify as a character witness, though I don't know if I can do you any good."

"Do you know who the judge will be?"

"Judge V. Ellis Unger, most likely. He's tough, he's hell on wheels when his bile's up, but fair, straight, and knows his law. One thing, I don't know whether you prefer it or not, but I doubt if you'll get a jury trial."

"I'm entitled to one."

"In the States you are. Up here the procedures are all a little different. Corners are easily cut. Law enforcement is stretched pretty thin throughout the territory. The crime rate is discouragingly high. The courts are overwhelmed. The dispensation of justice has to be sped up. Judges can hear and decide six cases a day or more. When a jury's involved, a trial can take a week."

"So it's a matter of expediency."

"I guess you can say that. Still, if I were you, I'd rather have Unger decide my fate than twelve strangers. Oh, I guess you could insist on a jury trial, but it might not be in your best interests to."

"I'd be alienating his honor."

Meriweather bobbed his head from side to side, suggesting to Horne that his assumption was right. They said their good-byes and Meriweather left.

Horne had gotten a good look at Juneau on the walk from the dock to the jail in the center of town. Meriweather had pointed out the Governor's Mansion and the Baranof Hotel. The town appeared to be eight times the size of Skagway and far more civilized: no gunfire in the streets, no drunken sourdoughs staggering about, no fistfighting or spontaneous shoot-outs.

When Meriweather left, T.G. sat in his newly acquired residence thinking, ignoring the soreness in his head. He had certainly reached the bottom rung. What, he wondered, lay below it? It was like being in a poker game with strangers with the cards stacked against you, down to your last handful of chips. It was disheartening. Lucien had robbed him of his money, his property, his pride, and most recently, the contents of his wallet. He didn't have a dime to hire a lawyer, and knowing the breed as he had come to over the years, not one would take his case without something on account. Lucien had stolen something else, something more precious than money and property: he'd taken from his self-esteem, along with his habitual optimism that he took such pride in, the intrinsic ability to see the bright side of the darkest situation. At the moment all in view was jet-black.

He sat mulling over his plight for about an hour, wondering among other things what Meriweather would do with his .45, his dagger-mounted knuckle-duster, .22 Sharps, and Barns boot pistol, when a familiar voice commanded his attention.

"T.G."

"Perry!"

Marshal Sinatra unlocked the door and let him in. He returned to his post and left them alone."

"I thought you were on the way to San Antonio."

"I was. On the boat coming down from Skagway, I—"

"Had second thoughts."

"Something like that. I stopped off here, took a room, bought both the local newspapers, and caught upon your exploits. So it blew up in your face, after all. As I predicted."

"Don't start gloating, I don't need it. None of this would had happened if you hadn't deserted me."

"Oh, then I'm to blame."

"You're entitled to your share."

"Enlighten me, please. The more imaginative types of fiction have always fascinated me."

"I mean it. If you'd come to the store with me like you promised, you'd have been standing lookout outside. He would have seen you, wouldn't have dared knock me cold with the safe door."

"How, dear boy, could I have prevented it?"

"He would have naturally assumed you were armed, and if he tried anything, you'd come storming in and—"

"Plug him through the head."

"Right."

"Balderdash. Why didn't you pay attention to what you were doing? You had the drop on him. Why did you take your eyes off him? What would anybody do but swing the door and knock you out?"

"He nearly brained me."

"Serves you right."

"Oh, shut up! You want to hear the last straw, the crusher? After he knocked me out he picked my pocket."

"Gracious."

"Yeah, gracious."

"Bad luck. So that's another seventeen hundred you're out. Flush or broke, you're going to need a lawyer. We'll have to locate somebody you can borrow from—"

"At thirty-five percent? Fifty? How about a hundred?"

"My goodness, that would be usury. Don't be an ingrate; my patience only stretches so far. It may interest you to know I've already been working on your behalf. I've made preparations to engage the most capable attorney available to defend you."

"Did I tell you I'm suing DeBlois?"

"First things first. Let's see what can be done to keep you out of durance vile. You're to be defended by Attorney Agatha Trent Woodward, known among her enemies as Glass-eye Aggie."

"A woman—"

"Does that bother you?"

"No."

"Then please don't interrupt. She hasn't agreed to take your case just yet. She naturally wants to discuss it with you first before making up her mind, but I see no reason why she won't get on board. Do you? Good. She's waiting outside. She usually commands a hundred dollars out front in grand-larceny cases, murders, suchlike, but I think I can get her down to fifty. I'll just turn up the power on the old Youngquist charm. I can already see from the way she looks at me when she's listening she's attracted to me."

"How old is she?"

"What do you ask that for?"

"If she's attracted to you she's got to be in her dotage."

"Don't be snide. I'm here to help, not to be insulted." He clapped his hands on his bony knees. "Well, then, shall I bring the lady in?"

"I guess."

"Please, don't be so enthusiastic."

"What have I got to be enthusiastic about? I've been robbed blind, suckered like a greenhorn, insulted, ridiculed. I'm being railroaded—"

"Stop feeling sorry for yourself. Buck up, be thankful I got off here instead of staying on to Portland. Tidy up a bit, straighten your tie, button your vest, comb your hair with your fingers, and be a gentleman."

*   *   *

Perry had not described Lawyer Woodward physically so Horne was ill-prepared for the sight that met his eyes. She was built along the lines of a whistle-stop water tower minus the supporting structure. Her bosom was startlingly formidable; at first sight of it he pictured a man lying prone behind her cleavage, defending himself with a rifle against attacking outlaws. He would be in no danger of being hit with such cover. She looked to be a few weeks north of fifty, with chestnut hair chopped off two inches from her shoulders and in bangs over her functioning eye and its glass companion. Glass-eyed she was, but unlike other glass eyes he'd seen that stared blankly, hers seemed to have life and light lurking behind the iris. She fixed it on him, practically pinning him to the wall at his back. Her voice was cavernously deep and had a cutting edge to it, like that of a reprimanding schoolmaster, not marm. She conveyed the impression physically as well as audibly of assuming complete charge thirty seconds after she entered the cell. She carried a briefcase and out of it brought a legal pad and gold-filled mechanical pencil.

"Name?"

"T.G. Horne."

"Age?"

"Thirty-three."

He answered every question promptly, not daring to hesitate. He provided her his physical measurements. He began getting the feeling that she wanted them on the record to select the right size coffin. Marshal Sinatra exuded no warmth; Lawyer Woodward exuded a sort of damp coldness, filling the little cell with it. He told his story.

"That's it?"

"That's it."

"This is exactly as it happened, right? You're not gussying it up to make him look bad and you better."

"That's exactly what happened."

"Whatever possessed you to barge in on him like that?"

"He went off half-cocked," began Perry.

She turned and glared at him. He shrank slightly and mumbled an apology.

"I . . . " began Horne. "We'd come a long way. I was angry; it had all been building up inside me since the night he attacked me in my hotel room. I didn't like him the first time I laid eyes on him. I—"

"Made a stupid mistake. Idiotic. You're not going to hang for it, but they can put you away for a Christmas or two. Don't look so hangdog, you're in luck: hapless innocents who blunder into breaking the law are my weakness."

"Then you'll take the case?"

"My fee is five hundred if I get you off, one hundred if I don't. Out front."

"Miss Woodward, Agatha—may I call you Agatha?" purred Perry. "We've come a long long way; it's been arduous, it's been expensive. Frankly, I'm practically tapped out. T.G. is. Could you, would you find it in your heart to, er, make allowances for our situation."

Her face cracked, breaking into the most lascivious smile Horne had seen in ages. Perry smiled in response.

"I understand, Pericles, extenuating factors. I suppose fifty will do. Of course, if I do you a favor, that gives me the right to expect one in return, doesn't it?"

Before Perry could answer, she reached over, seized his hand, squeezed it, and winked her good eye suggestively.

My God, mused Horne, he was right. She's after his bones. He studied Perry; he didn't appear worried. What was running through his mind? he wondered. Was he planning to lead her on, pretend to be interested, and milk her attraction to him for what could be gotten out of it, short of going to bed with her? He couldn't do that. She'd break him in two; she outweighed him by eighty pounds; she'd either crush him to death or strain his heart until it gave out.

She rose to her feet still clinging to Perry's hand. "That's all I need for now. We'll be on our way."

"Be back later," said Perry.

"Much later," she sang, and to Horne's surprise, she bussed Perry soundly on the cheek. He grinned self-consciously, waved, and they left. And that, reflected Horne, was that. Welcome to Juneau, meet your lawyer: the greatest man-eater in history since Cleopatra, with traces of Lucrezia Borgia tossed in. Was she as capable as Perry made her out to be earlier, or was his judgment clouded by the boost to his vanity?

He was seventy-two; he probably hadn't slept with a woman in ten years. Could he? Would he be up to her demands? The word "voracious" popped into mind, followed by insatiable. Would he survive and conquer?

Would he survive at all?

11

Attorney Woodward came alone to see her client the next morning. She looked to Horne like a cat who had just finished a saucer of fresh cream, a politician who had just learned that he'd won a close and critical election, a satisfied bride on the morning of her wedding night. For all her lack of beauty she glowed. Sight of her emotional state struck fear into his heart.

"Where's Perry?"

"When I left him he was asleep. I think . . ."

"What!"

"Asleep. He wasn't stirring; he seemed to be dreaming. He had the cutest smile on his face, the dear. Why what's wrong?"

"Nothing."

"You're worried about your case, of course. Well, I've given a good deal of thought to it, examined it from every angle."

"And?"

"Unquestionably you're the injured party. Our problem is proving it. You have no witnesses to his attack on you in the hotel room. I'll be honest. From what I can see it'll be impossible to prove your story."

"My God . . ."

"What we'll have to do is turn the thing around and try to disprove your accuser's. Now, you claim the brother behind the counter wasn't Louis but Lucien."

"Definitely. I'd stake my life on it."

"Don't be in such a hurry to. If it was Lucien you talked to, then you've yet to meet Louis. How can you make a comparison?"

"He came to my cell up in Skagway and admitted he was Lucien."

"Did you think he was telling the truth?"

"Of course! Why would he lie?"

"He might. Some people have a sadistic streak a mile wide. Still, if it was Lucien, he doesn't risk anything telling you. He knows that in court if he has to go up on the stand it'll be his word against yours."

"It was Lucien!"

"All right. But there were no witnesses in the hotel room, none in the store; so, as I say, it's his word against yours. And since you're the aggressor—"

"Not back in Hurdlesford. If I'm guilty of anything it's retaliation. Have you been able to find out where Louis has gotten to? He seems to have conveniently disappeared into thin air."

"I'm working on that. If we're going to stand a Chinaman's chance, we'll need both of them in court and up on the stand. Of course, the prosecution will do its damnedest to keep Lucien from testifying. They'll argue he wasn't in the store, that he has nothing to do with Louis' brief against you."

"He has everything to do with it!" He sighed. "I don't understand it. What was he doing posing as Louis? You think because he expected I'd show up and figured he'd be better able to handle me? And wanted to, couldn't pass up the opportunity? Why would Louis let Lucien pose as him? Meriweather says they hate each other."

"I wouldn't be too sure. Oh, I know all about Louis' wife's alleged fascination with Lucien, that husband and wife are at odds over dear brother, but that doesn't necessarily mean Louis hates him or that they hate each other. I know, one is a sterling character, respected in the community, and the other's the black sleep of the family, but being different is no grounds for hatred. And they *are* twins, the next best thing to being joined at the hip. Twins can be unnaturally close, which makes sense. Each does see the other in his own image. A little like stepping out of your body, moving a few feet away, and seeing yourself. No matter how much Louis may disapprove of Lucien's deportment, particularly his interest in his wife, he probably wouldn't turn his back on him when Lucien asks for help."

"Blood is thicker than gall."

"Something like that."

"Marion's the unknown quantity. We really don't know how Louis feels toward her; it's possible he couldn't care less if she wants to fool around with his brother. Possibly he doesn't even know about it—or if he does, blames her."

"It'll all come out in court, and could help us."

"I hope."

"We go to trial in three days."

"That soon?"

"The wheels of justice grind fast up here. They have to, otherwise we'd have a backlog of cases as big as the Mendenhall Glacier." She paused and good-eyed him. "I must tell you, we do have a new problem."

"Oh, my God."

"Take it easy. My stars, you are a nervous Nellie, aren't you? I know this mess is tremendously upsetting, frustrating; you're not to blame for a blessed thing and here you're catching it from all sides. But courting a heart attack from stress isn't going to help. The problem I'm speaking of isn't insurmountable."

"Tell me."

"If you'll relax and stop bracing yourself, I will. I heard this morning that Judge Unger has removed himself from the case. He's left town with the governor. They've gone down to Seattle and won't be back till next week. Judge Woodward is taking Unger's place."

"Woodward? Any relation?"

"My older sister, Miriam."

"Terrific!"

"Maybe not." She was suddenly looking at him strangely, prompting a sinking feeling.

"You don't get along—"

"We despise each other."

"My God."

"Don't jump to conclusions. She only resents me as a person, not as a lawyer. She's a first-rate judge, as good if not better than Unger. But—and consider this fair warning—the one thing she will not tolerate is deceit. It sends her flying off the handle faster than greased lightning. And she can smell it like a she-wolf smells musk four miles away. Even a hint of lying or evasion, of trying to cover up, even indecisiveness when a clear-cut answer is in order and she'll come down on you like falling rocks.

"Now, as honest and straightforward as you may be, it can happen under the stress of the proceedings that you inadvertently hedge or perhaps contradict yourself or unwittingly bend the truth. You're going to have to steel yourself against that; weigh every syllable before you utter it. Can you do that?"

"I'll try."

"Don't try, just do it. Okay, let's rehearse the prosecutor's questions. It's easy enough to figure what he'll ask, nine questions out of ten. But be prepared for surprises and think before you respond. Nobody's going to rush you. I'll object till I'm red in the face if they try."

"You and your sister really dislike each other?"

"I said despise. But in court we both manage to control our feelings. Behave like professionals. It's a long story. You wouldn't be interested."

"I didn't think it was legal for one member of a family to sit in judgment when another member is representing one of the people."

"In the States, no. In Alaska nobody's ever cared. We're a people with rough edges; you should have noticed that by now. I've defended cases before her.

She won't have any prejudice against you because I'm your lawyer, if that's what you're worrying about."

"I'm worrying about everything. What did I ever do to deserve this? It must have been something indescribably horrible."

"I'm sure. Whatever you do, don't feel sorry for yourself. Okay, let's get busy on the questions."

12

"Your Honor, we intend to prove that the accused called on my client, Mr. Louis Jean DeBlois, for the express purpose of robbing him. Every aspect of the situation without exception underscores premeditation. To begin with, the accused waited until just before closing time to enter the premises, pausing outside to make certain no other patrons were present or approaching. He then entered, locked the door, and pulled the shades. I call your Honor's attention to the weapons accused carried, weapons taken from him by Deputy Marshal John Meriweather when he was summoned to arrest him. Exhibit A, a forty-five-caliber revolver fully loaded. B, a twenty-two-caliber Sharps derringer fully loaded. A fifty-caliber Barns pistol loaded and concealed in a leg holster. A dagger-mounted knuckle-duster. Your Honor, one can't help wondering if he was preparing to rob my client or go to war."

There was loud laughter and gavel raping.

"Proceed, Counselor."

Attorney Alton Brackett, an owlish little man with an extraordinarily lofty opinion of himself and his abilities, paced back and forth before the table upon which the weapons and other items pertaining to the case were displayed, each wearing a large lettered tag.

"Accused entered the premises, immediately snatched my client's diamond stickpin from his shirtfront, and

demanded at gunpoint that he open the office safe and
empty it of its valuables. Or— and these were his exact
words—'I'll give you ten seconds to open that safe or so
help me God I'll blow your head off.' Faced with this
threat to his life, Mr. DeBlois had no choice but to
comply, whereupon the accused entered the office area
and aimed his weapon at Mr. DeBlois' head to ensure
his continued cooperation.

"Then, your Honor, a curious thing happened which
was to alter the accused's planned course of events and
save my client from certain death at his hands. The
accused caught sight of something gleaming inside the
safe; it so attracted him, it distracted him. He bent over
to examine it. When he did, Mr. DeBlois courageously
seized the initiative and slammed the safe door against
his head, knocking him out.

"That, in substance, is what happened. The accused
entered the premises with the sole intention of robbing
Mr. DeBlois. So well-armed was he for the purpose he
would have had no difficulty making good his threat to
'blow his head off,' should he refuse to accede to his
demands."

On droned Attorney Brackett, basking in the lime-
light, repeating himself ad nauseam, and carefully skip-
ping over factors that, taken in sum, could not have
helped but arouse the judge's suspicions that there was
more to the case than the simplified version detailed by
the speaker. To Horne's surprise and disappointment,
however, Agatha did not once interrupt him to object to
his exaggerated, distorted version of events.

When Brackett was done and resumed his seat beside his client, Agatha addressed the judge briefly in
response, noting that there was more to the case than
was meeting her worthy opponent's eyes and that she
would clarify specifically in due time.

Brackett then called, "Louis Jean DeBlois to the
stand."

Horne looked about the courtroom for perhaps the
twentieth time since arriving. There was no sign of the

other twin. Marion and her father—by how Horne was convinced it was he—were seated among the spectators. They had been when Horne came in, she with Monsoon the cat on her lap. She looked straight through Horne without a glimmer of recognition when he walked past. Mr. King hadn't even bothered to look.

Horne looked at Louis. It was Lucien, he was dead certain of it.

"State your name."

"Louis Jean DeBlois."

"Liar," rasped Horne.

"Ssssh." Agatha laid a hand on one arm, Perry on the other.

Under Brackett's questioning "Louis" told his story, dovetailing it neatly with his questioner's version earlier addressed to the court. Then Brackett struck out for new territory.

"Mr. DeBlois, after the accused entered, locked the door, and pulled the shades, what did he do?"

"Zee first theeng he deed was snatch my diamond steeckpeen from my shirtfront."

"Exhibit E, your Honor," said Brackett, holding up the stickpin. "And subsequently, when you opened the safe as he demanded and he noticed something gleaming in the rear, can you tell us please what that was?"

"My Jürgensen watch."

"Exhibit F, your Honor. Mr. DeBlois, would you mind telling us how this pin and watch came into your possession?"

"Zey were geeven me by my brother, Lucien."

"Did he tell you where he got them?"

"He deed not."

"Sneaked them out of hock behind my back," rasped Horne.

"Sssssh!"

Brackett continued questioning DeBlois, after which he turned him over to Agatha.

"No questions of this witness at this time, your Honor, but I request permission to recall him later."

"Granted."

Looking at the judge and at her sister, Horne could see a family resemblance. Their builds were similar and both wore the same hair style. Their features matched, but her Honor's voice was testy and her eyes suspicious, as if her temper were all wound up and she was ready to pounce at the slightest provocation. Strangely enough, like Agatha, she also sported a glass eye. Two glass eyes in the same family? Could they be inherited? It boggled the mind.

"Next witness, Alton."

"We have no more witnesses, your Honor. No one else was present during the robbery attempt."

"Counselor Woodward?"

"Your Honor, I call T.G. Horne."

Horne was sworn and seated, identified and questioned. He told his story, beginning in Hurdlesford. Brackett immediately objected, contending that what went on in Kansas between him and Lucien DeBlois had no bearing on the case. Agatha disagreed, pointing out that it provided the motive for Horne's actions. He resumed detailing events, taking pains to avoid all reference to McCaskill's pawnshop. Lucien's purchasing the watch and stickpin were perfectly legal, regardless of his motives. McCaskill was at fault for not hanging on to them for the seven days prescribed by law in Kansas. Brackett continued to interrupt, objecting that Lucien DeBlois was not involved in the case, he had no intention of summoning him as a witness, and "his worthy opponent" should not be allowed to drag him in by the heels. Agatha just as determinedly reminded him that it was his witness, Louis, who had introduced Lucien's name into the testimony.

She turned to Exhibit F. "Mr. Horne, we've heard Mr. DeBlois tell us under oath that this watch was a gift from his brother. Purchased by Lucien, given to him. You maintain it's your watch. Can you prove it is?"

"My initials are inside the back."

"Are you sure?"

"Absolutely."

The judge gestured. Agatha handed the watch to her. "Would your Honor read the initial inside the back?"

"T.G.H.," interposed Horne.

The judge opened the watch and read, "L.D.B."

"Lucien or Louis DeBlois!" burst Brackett exultantly.

Horne saw red. He exploded. "Impossible!" Half-rising from the witness chair, he thrust out his hand to snatch the watch from the judge. She held it out of reach like an older boy teasing, holding a ball away form a younger one.

"Sit down and quiet down or I'll hold you in contempt."

"Your Honor, that's my watch. My initials were inside the back. The back's been changed, it must have been—"

"This is a Jürgensen watch," said the judge. "Not terribly common, but common enough. I've seem them before. And to these eyes it's impossible to distinguish one from another."

"The back's been changed," Horne persisted.

"I heard you the first time. Half the town did. Prove it."

"Your Honor," said Agatha, "may we put the watch to one side for the moment?"

"What have you got in mind, Counselor?"

"With the court's permission I'd like to concentrate on Exhibit E, the diamond horseshoe stickpin."

"Proceed."

Agatha held the stickpin before Horne. "You both claim ownership of this. I ask you, Mr. Horne, can you prove it belongs to you?"

"My initials are on it. Inside."

Brackett gasped aloud. Wide-eyed, he swung about and glowered at DeBlois. Judge Woodward gestured for the stickpin. It was handed up to her.

"Just two initials," continued Horne. "The T is superimposed over the H: three vertical lines, two horizontal, one at the top, the other through the center. You'll find them inside the little rounded pin clasp. They're tiny, practically invisible to the naked eye."

Judge Woodward eyed him skeptically. "You're sure you're not wasting the court's time."

"They're there; you'll need a magnifying glass."

She snapped her fingers at the bailiff.

"In my chambers, Horace, bottom right desk drawer."

Off sprinted the bailiff. The judge let the spectators rumble among themselves while everyone waited. Back came the bailiff holding a small silver magnifying glass aloft as if it were the Olympic torch. The judge rapped for order and examined the pin clasp under the glass. There was a long, trenchant silence during which Brackett continued to start daggers at his client. DeBlois looked embarrassed and refused to meet his eyes. Horne held his breath and Marion stroked the cat in her lap. Judge Woodward cleared her throat. The spectators leaned forward expectantly.

"T.H.," she declared.

The spectators erupted; she gaveled for order and handed the pin back to Agatha, who set it among the other exhibits.

"That's good enough for me," said the judge. "The pin's yours, Mr. Horne. The watch is yours, Mr. DeBlois."

"Your Honor," said Agatha, "before you make a final decision as to the rightful ownership of either piece, I would like to postpone further questioning for Mr. Horne and bring another witness to the stand. And after him, recall Mr. Horne."

"Alton?"

Brackett gestured theatrically, granting his permission.

"Mr. Voltaire Murgtaugh," said Agatha.

Voltaire Murtaugh was infinitely less impressive in appearance than his famous namesake. He was runty, gnarled as a walnut, with a shock of yellow-white hair that fountained upward from the summit of his brow, and eyes that pierced even more sharply than did Perry's.

"Mr. Murtaugh, will you tell us what you do for a living?"

"Horologist."

"A . . ."

"I make and vend clocks and watches."

"And how long have you been in this profession?"

"Thirty-two years."

"You're an expert."

"I'm considered to be."

"So expert the governor entrusts all the clocks in the mansion and his personal timepieces to your care. You have written testimonials to your expertise from some of the best-known—"

"Your Honor," interrupted Brackett, "we'll accept him as an expert. No point in wasting the court's time."

Agatha held up the watch. "Have you ever seen this watch before, Mr. Murtaugh?"

"I can't say, I'd have to examine it."

She handed it to him. He screwed a jeweler's loupe into his eye, adding more gnarls to his wizened face. He inspected the watch inside and out for fully two minutes before handing it back.

"I've never seen it before."

"You've heard Mr. Horne's testimony. He claims this is his, and yet Mr. DeBlois' initials are inside the back. Mr. Horne insists the back with his initials on it has been removed and this back substituted."

"Obviously, I can hardly attest to whether the original back was or wasn't engraved, but he's right about one thing: that isn't it. That back is new."

The spectators stirred, the gavel rapped.

"How can you tell?" Agatha asked.

"Easy." She returned the watch to him. He opened the back, exposing the dome. "This is what we call American gold; it's got copper in it. That's what gives it its reddish cast. This replacement back is also American gold, but it's newer than the rest of the case. It's been bathed in a solution that ages it years in a few hours to make it look like it matches the case. The layman probably wouldn't notice the difference. I can see it easily, even without my glass. Trick of the trade, bath-aging. It's an excellent fit, but there's that unmistakable shade of difference in the colors. Compare it with the dome and you can see. Also, the joint—"

"Joint?" asked the judge.

"What you'd call the hinge, your Honor. It has three sleeves. The ones at either end attached to the case; the center one attaches to the back. Under the glass you can see the slight difference in color the same as be-tween the back and the dome. Also, whoever rein-serted the pin was a bit hasty. A tool called a joint-pusher is used; whoever pushed that pin back made two tiny scratch marks. No watch from a reputable watchmaker ever shows scratch marks. It's definitely not the origi-nal back. I'd stake my reputation on it."

"Thank you, Mr. Murtaugh."

"Counselor," the judge asked Brackett, "any ques-tions?" Again Brackett flung his hand flamboyantly, dis-missing the question without speaking. "I asked you a question," said the judge sternly. "Kindly have the courtesy to respond."

"No questions, your Honor, no questions at all," he stammered. "Thank you. Sorry, I apologize."

"The witness is excused," said the judge.

Agatha turned toward her sister. "Your Honor, the fact that Mr. Horne was correct, that a new back has been substituted for the original doesn't establish that the original bore his initials. It does, however, cast into serious doubt Mr. DeBlois' claim of ownership."

"Possibly," said the judge. "Still, it could have be-longed to someone other than either, a third party. When it came into Mr. DeBlois' possession, it would be natural for him to replace the original owner's initials with his own."

"Agreed, your Honor."

"I said earlier it's impossible to distinguish one Jürgensen watch from another. For anyone other than Mr. Murtaugh. I'm speaking, of course, of the original

DOUBLE TROUBLE IN SKAGWAY

watch, not one that's been altered in any way as this one has."

"True, your Honor, but if we associate the stickpin with the watch, taking them so to speak as two parts of the whole, the picture takes on a different light. Mr. DeBlois has testified that he is the owner of the stickpin purchased from him by his brother. And yet you yourself confirmed that the stickpin bears Mr. Horne's initials. And he claims the watch also bore his initials."

"You have a point, Counselor."

"I object, your Honor. My worthy opponent is inundating us with assumptions in lieu of facts. Everybody knows much of the jewelry in the country sold over the counter is previously owned. Mr. DeBlois' brother purchased both these items in good faith. It's possible they were sold to him in bad faith, touted as being brand-new."

"Is that an assumption, Alton, or a fact?"

"I . . . I . . ."

"The watch could hardly pass for new; anyone can see it's worn. But tell me something. Do you mean to imply that the initials T H on the stickpin in Mr. DeBlois' possession is a coincidence?"

"Ah . . ."

She rapped her gavel. "Mr. DeBlois, take the stand."

The witness already sworn, Judge Woodward questioned him.

"When the watch came into your possession and you opened the back the first time, what initials did you see there?"

"Ah . . . none, your Honor."

"No initials?"

"Ah, no."

"But you had the back changed. Why? Why bother? If it wasn't initialed, why didn't you just have yours put on?"

"Ah, eet was dented, your Honor."

"Dented."

"And badly scratched. I thought eet best to replace eet."

"Liar," rasped Horne.

"Ssssh!"

The judge was studying DeBlois, saying nothing further for the moment. He had started to sweat. His eyes darted about like those of a cornered animal. He flushed, then blurted forth. "What deeference does eet make who zey belong to; zey are legally mine! Zey came from a pawnshop een Hurdlesford, Kansas." He pointed at Horne. "He hock zem, Lucien was weetheen hees rights to buy zem. Zey are mine. Mine!"

A soft, warm wave of smugness rolled over Horne; he settled deeper in his chair, relaxed, and smiled. The cat was out of the bag at last.

"Objection! With all due respect, your Honor, I fail to see where any of this is leading us. One would think Mr. DeBlois is on trial. He's the injured party."

"He's also a witness, and I expect witnesses under oath to be forthright. And there's no need to remind this court who is what. You prefaced this case by telling us what happened in Mr. DeBlois' place of business when Mr. Horne came there. He arrived heavily armed to rob Mr. DeBlois, he threatened him, but Mr. DeBlois was able to turn the tables on him

"We have also heard Mr. Horne's version of the incident, and what preceded it in Kansas, which the defense would have us believe motivated his action. Interestingly, there seem to be more and more aspects to this thing coming to light every few minutes. You're excused, Mr. DeBlois; Mr. Horne, take the stand."

Horne did so. Under the judge's questioning he recounted the poker game, pointing out that Lucien DeBlois had lost heavily and had left the table practically broke, with not nearly enough money to meet Horne's bluff raise of five thousand dollars. Had he elected to, he would have had to play light. He declined to do so and took his loss. Yet only five hours later, early the next morning, he was sufficiently flush to purchase a thousand-dollar watch, and eight-hundred dollar stickpin, and buy a train ticket to San Francisco. Having taken a firm grip on the bull's horns, Horne began squeezing, recognizing that DeBlois' vacillating, his concealing his knowledge of the pawnshop, and Murtaugh's testimony had combined to turn the tide in his favor. He was determined to keep it flowing in that direction. He repeated his earlier testimony that he had identified Lucien DeBlois without actually seeing him by his eau de cologne. Brackett leapt on this almost gleefully, poohpoohing it and ridiculing him. But Judge Woodward, being a woman, held the orange blossoms in higher regard as a means for identification. She informed Brackett that there probably wasn't a woman among the spectators who couldn't recognize at least one friend or acquaintance by her perfume.

When she had finished enlightening him on this point, she consulted her watch. It was four o'clock.

"Court's adjourned until ten tomorrow morning. We will hear any further testimony, Alton and Counselor Woodward will deliver their summations, and I shall render my verdict."

13

Louis DeBlois' uncertainty and somewhat question-able behavior on the witness stand rubbed Judge Woodward the wrong way. The trial had reconvened at ten sharp the next morning and the proceedings were not three minutes old before it became obvious to Horne that her Honor was viewing his accuser through different, decidedly more skeptical eyes. The butter that previously wouldn't melt in his mouth had appeared to turn slightly rancid.

Nevertheless, his descent from grace did nothing to brighten Horne's chances. Brackett resumed arguing that the events involving him and Lucien back in Kansas that had prompted his visit to Louis' store were separate and distinct from that visit. Lucien's duplicity may have provided Horne with a motive, but that did not excuse his conduct and actions vis-à-vis Brother Louis.

True to his word Deputy Marshal Meriweather showed up, took the stand, and was questioned by Agatha. He corroborated Horne's earlier testimony, saying that Horne had told him he was absolutely certain that it was Lucien behind the counter. Unfortunately, in cross-examination, Brackett was able to elicit the deputy's own opinion in this regard.

"Mr. DeBlois summoned you to his premises to arrest Mr. Horne. When you got there, was there the slightest doubt in your mind that it wasn't Louis who greeted you?"

"It was Louis."

"You know both brothers?"

"For years."

"Despite their being identical twins, you know one from the other."

"I do. There's a lot that's different about them."

"And when you got there, it was Louis behind the counter."

"Yes."

"No further questions, your Honor."

No further testimony was heard. Judge Woodward called for Counselor Brackett's summation. Since being chided by the judge for his histrionics, he had become less jaunty, less of a poseur.

"Your Honor, this case revolves around one specific incident, only one: the accused's visit to my client's place of business and what went on during that visit. Accused came armed to the teeth. My worthy opponent has pointed out that Mr. Horne is a professional gambler and such individuals are accustomed to carrying more than one weapon. Let me point out, however, that he didn't go into the store to play poker. He went in to get the sixty thousand dollars he claims Lucien DeBlois stole from him. When Louis DeBlois properly identified himself, Horne refused to believe he was Lucien's twin, ignoring his every attempt to explain, and threatened him with his life if he did not 'pay up.' Even before demanding the money, he brazenly snatched Mr. DeBlois' diamond stickpin from his shirtfront.

"As things turned out, as we have all heard, Mr. DeBlois alertly turned the tables on Horne, banged the safe door against his head, and knocked him out, then summoned the law. Successful though he was in thwarting the robbery attempt and saving his life, Mr. DeBlois has suffered greatly from the experience. Indeed, were he not in excellent health—if, God forbid, he had a weak heart—he well might have perished on the spot as

a result of the terrible stress inflicted upon him by
Horne. As it is, his doctor prescribed medicine he must
take religiously three times daily for his nerves. And his
sleep has been disturbed by nightmares.

"We have heard Deputy Marshal Meriweather's testimony; he told us that he has no trouble distinguishing
between Lucien and Louis, even though they're identical twins. Nor, I'm certain, does anyone else acquainted
with them. Horne met Lucien in Hurdlesford, Kansas,
followed him to Skagway, and entered Louis' store to
confront Louis, he would have us believe, mistaking
him for Lucien. I for one cannot accept this; I believe
that he entered the store, and when Louis identified
himself, denying he was Lucien, Horne conveniently
disregarded his explanation and proceeded with his attempt to rob him. I believe that once inside the store,
perceiving it to be a large and evidently successful
business, he resolved not to leave without taking his
sixty thousand dollars. Whichever brother was behind
the counter mattered not. He had come all the way
from Kansas and was determined to get his money, and
he was not particular about who gave it to him. Granted,
he had never met Louis before entering the store, but
he did know Lucien. One might even say intimately.
Had spent hours playing poker with him, had seen him,
so to speak, with his hair down. Deputy Marshal
Meriweather has testified as to how easy it is to distinguish between the two brothers. Despite the fact that
Horne had never met Louis, knowing as he did, it is
preposterous that he failed to see the difference. Preposterous, your Honor, and that alleged failure is the
core of his defense of his actions. His only defense. I for
one refuse to accept that. I say he entered the store to
get his money and that if you or I or anyone had been
behind the counter in place of Louis DeBlois, Horne
would not have hesitated an instant. He would have
treated you or me, anyone, as ruthlessly, as viciously,
as he treated Louis.

"I ask that the court consider him in the full light of

his criminal behavior, that there is no room for leniency. He attempted robbery, he threatened to kill his victim if his demands were not met; he should be made to pay for his actions to the fullest extent of the law. I thank you."

"Thank you, Alton. Counselor Woodward . . ."

"Your Honor, I should like if I may to attempt to put all of us in Mr. Horne's place at the time and site of the incident involving him and Mr. DeBlois. Mr. Horne had come approximately twenty-five hundred miles, traveling every mile every click of the rails with the fires of resentment burning in his bosom. He had been set upon and robbed and he pursued his attacker, fortunately able to—he wasn't murdered for his money—all the way to Skagway.

"His attacker also in effect stole his prize watch and stickpin both, as we have seen, engraved with his initials. I ask you to put yourself in Mr. Horne's place. You walk into DeBlois' store and there, standing behind the counter, is Mr. DeBlois. Not Mr. Lucien DeBlois, but Louis. Up to now you don't even know Louis DeBlois exists. To you, understandably, to anyone who doesn't know, the man behind the counter is Lucien DeBlois. The fire in your bosom flares at sight of him; the first object you see is your diamond horseshoe stickpin displayed on Mr. DeBlois' shirtfront. You see it, you see red. Crimson! You see blood! You snatch it from him. You demand your money. He tries to explain that it is Lucien whom you want, not him. He tells you they are twins.

"Do you believe him? You do not, you're too outraged to think clearly. Besides, the explanation—to use my worthy opponent's word—is preposterous. Much too convenient. Twins? Ridiculous. Mr. DeBlois insists he's telling the truth, but all he's succeeding in doing is making you angrier. You become incensed, you demand the money that is rightfully yours, but he tells you he only has a few hundred on hand. Why should he pay you a cent? He's not the one who owes you. Unfortunately, his offer only underscores your skepticim, your unwillingness to accept his explanation that he is one of twin brothers. The wrong one.

"He opens the safe and practically the first thing you see is a strongbox that turns out to be filled with money. Only a few hundred? Then you see something gleam at the back of the second shelf. Your heart beats faster: it's your watch. You kneel for a closer look. He slams the door against your head; fortunately, very very fortunately, not killing you, not fracturing your skull.

"You wake up in jail. You are not in jail an hour before who should come by but Mr. DeBlois. From the other side of the bars he taunts you, laughs at your frustration, telling you what you have suspected all along, that he is Lucien, not Louis. Dares you to tell anyone, confident that no one will believe you, not one will take the word of a stranger against his word.

"You've come all this way to end up not only empty-handed, but severely injured, arrested, jailed, and on trial. For what? For attempting to recover what is rightfully yours, only yours. This case, your Honor, in every aspect, from every angle, by way of every possible interpretation is a classic travesty on justice. Laws are formulated to protect the innocent, people who have been wronged, made to suffer unjustifiably, illegally deprived of their money, property, and peace of mind. Mr. Horne has been treated unjustly, outrageously so. Shamefully. All we ask is that the justice denied him up to this moment be granted him, that the charges be dropped and he be allowed to go free and his property returned. Thank you."

Judge Woodward waited a long moment before speaking, then cleared her throat, eyed Louis DeBlois, then eyed Horne.

"Mr. Horne, you will approach and stand before the bench. I have decided upon a verdict in this case. It has not been an easy decision to reach. Counselor Woodward is quite right in her references to your inconvenience, the unfairness with which you've been treated, your mental anguish, and much else. However, Counselor Brackett has touched on the pivotal factor in this case, and the court concurs with his interpretation of it, his evaluation of it. Namely, what transpired back in Kansas has no bearing whatsoever on what happened in Skagway.

"Mr. Horne, I can believe that when you entered the store you had no intention of browbeating whoever you encountered inside, but when you came face to face with Louis DeBlois, unaware that he is one of twins and an innocent victim of circumstances, shall I say formulated by his brother Lucien, you mistook him for Lucien, threatened him, and tried to rob him.

"Understand something, Mr. Horne: when you walked in, Louis had no way of knowing who you were, no way of knowing what eventuated between you and his brother. He accepted the watch and stickpin from Lucien in all innocence, probably not questioning where they had come from. Who among us looks a gift horse in the mouth?

"What you did, what you attempted, you did not to Lucien but to Louis. Under existing territorial law I could find you guilty and sentence you to two to four years in prison. But Counselor Woodward has pleaded your case, your side of this unfortunate affair, eloquently and persuasively. There is no question in my mind but that there have been many extenuating factors. I have heard you testify, and in spite of your admitted occupation, I do not consider you the criminal type. You're no run-of-the-mill holdup man. However, you did attempt to hold up Mr. DeBlois. I therefore find you guilty and sentence you to two years' incarceration, sentence suspended. I hold you liable for damages in the sum of one dollar payable to the bailiff upon leaving this courtroom. As to your watch and stickpin, I find them to be the legal property of Louis DeBlois, purchased and paid for by his brother and given to him."

Gavel rapped.

"This case is officially closed. Next case."

14

Paying the dollar for damages to the bailiff was difficult for Horne; the simple gesture invited as much pain and suffering as the safe door meeting his head. To make matters worse, in full view of the amused DeBlois, husband and wife, and father-in-law King, he had to borrow the dollar from Perry. Attorney Brackett was not amused; he had been out for blood, and Judge Woodward's decision, suspending the two-year sentence, vexed him greatly.

Horne, Perry, and Agatha adjourned to the restaurant across the street. Horne had plunged into the doldrums.

Perry ordered coffee for the three of them. "Why so down?" he asked. "You don't have to go to prison; I should think you'd at least be relieved."

"I'm rescinding the balance of my fee, T.G.," said Agatha. "That should perk you up a bit. We managed to keep you out of prison, but the final results were mixed at best. I do wish we could have gotten back your watch and stickpin; that would at least be a token triumph. T.G., are you listening?"

"Mmmmm."

"T.G., thank the lady."

"Thank you. I want to pay the four-fifty regardless. And hire your services. I'm going to sue that son of a bitch."

124

Perry scoffed. "Don't be ridiculous. That was Louis, he doesn't owe you a red cent."

"It was Lucien, dammit!"

"I still don't see how you can tell one from the other without ever having laid eyes on the other," said Agatha. "John Meriweather was on your side up on the stand; he tried, but you can hardly expect him to lie under oath."

"You don't understand, either of you. He gave a clear picture of the differences between them. The Lucien he described on the stand and back up in Skagway was behind the counter. Everything about him tallies."

"To your satisfaction, perhaps."

"No perhaps about it."

Agatha shrugged. "If you say so. But for you to sue—"

"Pay no attention," said Perry. "It's the bitterness talking."

"You'd be wasting your time," Agatha said.

"My boy," said Perry, "you gave it your best shot. And regardless of what you may think, I have to believe you got off lucky. Not being put away is certainly lucky."

"He took my money, my property, and emptied my wallet. And back there in the courtroom he laughed at me. You saw. Oh, not out loud, but laugh he did. So did she. So did her father."

"Forget about it."

Horne raised his head and fastened his eyes on Perry what a malevolent glare. "Forget about it? Never!" He slammed the table. "Never!"

"Ssssh, for pity's sakes."

"I'm going back to Skagway."

Perry bristled. "No you're not!"

"Try to stop me. I'm going to get my money and my things."

"He's right. T.G., listen to him. Going back there is the worst thing you could do. You get within ten yards

of Louis and he'll scream bloody murder. You'll find
yourself back in jail, back in the soup. He'll accuse you
a second time of threatening him, and whoever you
appeared before—my sister, Judge Unger—when the
dust clears, you'll be done for. There won't be any
suspended sentence a second time. There'll be two
years and the first two tacked on."

"Is that what you really want?" Perry asked. "Four
years behind bars?"

Horne was only half-listening. His mind was in a
rolling boil. Again he saw the taunting expressions on
the DeBlois' faces, saw his hand laying down the dollar
bill, heard their inaudible gibing laughter. They were
luckier than they knew, he thought. Had he had a gun
handy he probably would have shot them.

No, he had to go back to Skagway. There was no way
he could resume his life, leave the area, and journey to
San Antonio to pick up at poker where he'd left off. He
saw no point in arguing with them about it, trying to
get them to see his side. They already did, but they
simply disagreed with him. They saw the risks as much
too great for the simple reward of satisfaction, which,
after all, was what he'd be going back after. The money
was just money, the watch and stickpin, as fond as he
was of both, mere geegaws, and replacable; but the
gratification entailed in putting things right, bother the
dangers, was too precious to pass up. He was only a
man. With but one life to spend on the planet, one trip
through, and any man worth the salt in his blood did
not permit others to walk on him, kick dirt in his face,
and laugh at him. If he owed it to anyone, anything, he
owed it to his manhood to properly square accounts.

Perry and Agatha were both studying him.

"Look at his wheels whirling," Perry rasped, irritably. "There's no talking sense to him now. He's
stone-deaf. What can you do in this world, my dear,
but try to advise friends, try to help, try to keep
them from running headlong into disaster under the

full steam of their emotions? You try, you fail, you give it up."

"You can do that much for me," said Horne sarcastically. "It's all I ask."

"Not all, T.G. We can't talk you out of going back into the lion's den, there's nothing either of us can say. There's just one thing."

Agatha nodded. "What are you going to use for money?"

"You'll lend me a couple thousand," replied Horne, focusing his attention on Perry.

"Me? Don't be too sure. You'll go back there and get eaten alive and wind up behind bars. You failed handsomely once, this time it'll be even easier; you'll fail again. You think I want that on my conscience? You're my flesh and blood, T.G., you think I want to go back to the States and go it alone? You think I could sleep nights knowing you were behind bars and I helped put you there? No, thank you; the bank is closed."

"Thanks, Perry."

"You're welcome." Horne stood up. "Where are you going?"

"What do you care?"

"T.G., you're upset. We understand, we sympathize. Sit, calm down. Drink your coffee. It'll relax you. Give yourself ten minutes, you'll feel loads better."

"I feel fine. Agatha, I want to thank you. You did a marvelous job, considering the little you had to work with. I'm grateful, I appreciate it more than I can ever put into words. I owe you four hundred fifty dollars; you'll get it. Not today, not tomorrow, but you will. I promise."

"I don't want it. T.G." Her face had taken on an expression that said he was her twelve-year-old and was hurt and desolate and she was concerned about him. "Sit, please."

"I can't, I've things to do that can't wait. Thank you again. And good-bye. Good-bye, Perry."

* * *

He was broke, hungry, had no place to stay, was a stranger in town with no friends left to turn to, no connections. He couldn't afford to stay in Juneau, but couldn't afford boat passage to leave. People he passed wandering about town appeared to look through him, as if he wasn't even there. He began to feel no longer human, no longer corporeal, but a sort of wraith of his former self floating about. He tried to recall the last time he'd been in such woefully straitened circumstances. He couldn't remember even feeling so utterly useless, valueless before; feeling discarded. He felt as if he'd just come back from the funeral of his optimism. It had died, murdered by the DeBlois, and been interred never to rise again. He walked by the Governor's Mansion, crossing Capitol Avenue and heading down Ninth Street to Gold Creek, which bisected the town. He crossed the little bridge to Glacier Avenue and stopped briefly by the Fred Harris and Joseph Juneau monuments, the two men who had first found gold in Alaska. He looked at them without really seeing them, then went back across the creek and up Willoughby.

He sat on a stone bench opposite the marshal's office and the jail where he'd been incarcerated. It was now the middle of the afternoon. He had eaten no breakfast, being too upset to even think of food. He sat in silent misery listening to his stomach gurgle. The bells of the Old Russian Church rang the hour of three out over the town.

He reflected on his situation; it was so bad it intimidated, even frightened. How much lower could he sink? People were approaching. He glanced to his right. His heart twisted and accelerated. It was Marion and her father and two others.

Louis and Lucien!

Both!

Both? So he was in town, after all, keeping clear of the court proceedings for obvious reasons, but here, probably waiting in a hotel room for the carnival to end and the victory celebration to begin. All four wore victory smiles, looked relaxed, walking on air. Marion had her arm through Louis'.

They all saw him at the same time; he looked away, feeling his cheeks tingle, wondering how he appeared to them: a well-dressed tramp down on his luck. He stared at their backs. At the corner they paused before turning it and laughed merrily. Marion only looked back at him, then was gone. He had noticed Louis was wearing the stickpin and watch.

Or was it Lucien? Had Louis given both back to him, having completed his performance? It occurred to Horne that he'd been wrong all along in his stubborn insistence that Louis had been Lucien behind the counter. Obstinacy certainly hadn't helped his case. Wrong, everybody else right. It was Louis he'd confronted, wearing his pin. Louis in court. Louis, Louis, Louis.

Worn out by the strain of the events of the past few days, he suddenly had difficulty keeping his eyes open. At last he could no longer do so. He slept and dreamed. Of food, a chateaubriand incredibly thick, expertly grilled, girdled with mashed potatoes and attended by fresh vegetables steaming in their juices. He ate every speck, washing it down with a spectacular bordeaux. Still he was hungry; a lobster pilaf was set before him, the flesh coarsely diced and lightly browned in butter, and encased in a mold of rice, swimming in white wine sauce. He ate every morsel of meat, every grain of rice. The empty plate vanished, its place taken by Escalopes de veau Brancas, a thin layer of *mirepoix* of vegetables cooked in butter, coated in egg and breadcrumbs and sautéed in clarified butter. Every forkful was sinfully delicious, an emperor's feast delivered to his taste by mistake.

He was starting on quails à la Monselet stuffed with a *salcipon* of truffles and foie gras when he felt something lightly touch his chest.

It woke him. A shabbily dressed stranger, his griz-

zled, red face caked with dirty sweat, eyes bloodred,
breath foul, was poking in his breast pocket. Horne
grabbed his wrist, clamping it tightly, forcing him to
release his fingers. He cried out and swore. A bill
fluttered to the ground; the man tore free and ran off
massaging his wrist and cursing.

"Come back here, you thieving . . ."

Horne was on his feet; he looked down. They lay a
bill showing its back. Amazement took hold, then puz-
zlement. He hadn't caught the fellow in the act of
putting it into his pocket. Someone else must have
while he was asleep. He picked it up. Under his flowing and wavy mane of Perrylike white hair Andy Jack-
son looked to his right—somewhat apprehensively,
thought Horne, as if recognizing an enemy standing too
close to him. Part of his left hand clutched his robes at
the bottom of the oval portrait. Each corner displayed
the number twenty.

"What the—"

Perry must have come by and stuck it in his pocket.
The trump had shown up, spotted the edge of it peek-
ing out, saw he was asleep, and . . . Twenty dollars.
Never had such a relatively meager sum looked like so
much. There were to be sure occasions in every man's
life when a hundred dollars could be treated with the
indifference accorded a single rumpled dollar, and vice
versa. This twenty falling into his lap now was like
inheriting a fortune.

He pocketed it, yawned, stretched, and looked about.
His stomach gurgled. Yes, he would eat, he was fam-
ished. But no chateaubriand, nothing expensive—ham
and eggs, just enough to quiet his innards and restore
his energy. The rest of the money he would put toward
his stake. He would canvas the local bars, query the
bartenders, find out where there would be a game that
evening.

Like a spark leaping from flint and steel into dry
straw, crackling softly, sending up a wisp of smoke,

optimism roused itself from its interment, springing to life like the phoenix of old. Sixteen, seventeen dollars' worth of chips was all he needed. By nine o'clock he'd be a couple hundred to the good; by midnight the entire table would be at his mercy, his chips stacks toppling tall; by two he'd be bedded down in the most luxurious suite in the Baranof Hotel.

And tomorrow morning he'd be on the first boat north.

15

The poker room was at the rear of the Juneau saloon. It was about twenty feet square with two barred windows high up and an iron wood stove squatting in one corner. The windows had faded gold curtains that were kept drawn. The walls were plastered brick, the woodwork varnished. A large round table covered with green beize occupied the center of the room and was surrounded by seven cane chairs. The table was lit by a large lamp hanging from the ceiling and shaded against the eyes of the players. Other chairs for kibitzers were scattered about and there were two brass spittoons for the convenience of the chewers in the gathering.

Horne arrived early, eager to play, and wanting to make certain he would be among the first seven candidates for the cane chairs. He was not prepared for the other players who followed him in. Four were local gentry; the fifth was, to his amazement, none other than her Honor, Judge Woodward. The sixth was Pericles Youngquist, accompanied by Agatha, who had come along to kibitz. Judge Woodward and Perry were as surprised at the sight of Horne as he was of them. He greeted the judge in gentlemanly fashion and Perry amiably.

"Thanks for the twenty dollars, Perry. It was very thoughtful of you. I'm ashamed to keep it, but it did keep me from starving and I can play."

"What are you talking about, my boy?"

"The twenty you slipped into my pocket while I was dozing."

"You're mistaken, I didn't slip you anything. I haven't even seen you since you left the restaurant."

Horne's eyes drifted to Agatha. She beamed and shook her head.

"Then who?"

"You must have a guardian angel," said Agatha.

Horne shook his head. "John Meriweather."

"The deputy marshal?"

"He's the only one left who could have."

Two new boxed and sealed decks of Hart's Squared Linen Eagle Nonpareils were provided. Judge Woodward won the deal with an ace.

"Seven-card stud, five-card stud, straight draw. Draw with the bug wild. Draw with deuces wild. Draw with both. No manhandling the discards."

Forced to play cautiously at least to begin with, Horne met only two antes in the first five hands. He won the sixth, straight draw, dropped out of the next one, and won the next two. In less than half an hour he managed to build his modest stake into better than a hundred dollars. He now felt secure and prepared to confront the evening. Continuing to play in strict conformity with his personal rules, he worked his holdings up to eight hundred and around that figure they hovered until about nine-thirty. Meanwhile, he finished assessing the skills of the others. Three of the four men were plungers—poor players who, like so many poor players, seemed to waver between rashness and conservativeness, playing recklessly immediately after they lost in order, one would presume, to make up their loss as quickly as possible, rather than to patiently wait for decent cards to come their way.

Judge Woodward played surprisingly well, cautiously, patiently, intelligently. Perry played his customary highly professional style.

The dealer's choice, the dealer being one of the four

locals, was seven-card stud, nothing wild. Horne speedily found himself head to head with Judge Woodward,
which was not a situation he would have preferred. Her
Honor flint-eyed him out of her one working orb as the
dealer gave them her fifth card, giving Horne a straight,
four to the eight. Judge Woodward showed three hearts.
Horne studied her up cards. If her hole cards were
hearts she would have a flush, beating him. She was
high with a king and checked.

"Two hundred," he said.

She called. His next card turned up a useless deuce.
She drew another heart. And bet two hundred. She had
played well up to now, but had suddenly, inexplicably,
become heedless. He deduced that she would have bet
her three hearts had she a fourth in the hole in the last
round, confident that she would draw the fifth one. She
did not have a fourth in the hole, therefore had checked
to him after the fifth round.

He raised her two hundred. She raised back. He
called. She wanted to make him think she had her
flush. He knew she did not. But even before the seventh card was dealt, she wanted him out.

When he drew his useless deuce and she her fourth
heart it made the twelfth heart to show itself. There
were now exactly fifteen cards left in the pack. That
made twenty-five cards that had not been exposed,
among them her two hole cards. Against this was only
one heart. So it was 24-1 she would not make her flush.
Unless, of· course, it was already made, which was
unlikely, the way she had played her hand.

Their last cards were dealt facedown. She bet five
hundred dollars. Horne had but two hundred left. He
glanced at Perry. Perry nodded.

"Call," said Horne. "Two hundred, drawing three
hundred light."

"Are you good for it?" she asked caustically.

"He is," Perry said.

At which point her bluff blew up in her face. She
held a four-flush in hearts. Horne reached for the pot.

She said nothing; she didn't have to speak; her expression spoke eloquently in volumes. It said: I should have sent you up; I'll get even with you if we have to play until next Christmas.

He tried not to look at her, sneaking only a quick peek. He had not wiped her out, but had taken her for close to a thousand in one hand.

By eleven o'clock, three of the original locals had dropped out and their chairs were taken by others, two of whom proceeded to lose heavily and got out before midnight. Judge Woodward played more conservatively, refrained from bluffing, or attempting to, and managed to hold her own. Perry played his customary steady game, but could not pull anything halfway decent and ended up losing heavily.

Horne reckoned he was ahead by close to six thousand dollars. It gave him a heady feeling. He had not won so consistently since long before Hurdlesford. Indeed, this night's luck was Hurdlesford's turned inside out. Back there nothing worked; here, everything. As he expected, inevitably, he found himself up against Perry. He did not relish the confrontation, liked it even less than going up against the judge, but could not back down. His hand was too promising, and in the back of his mind lurked the temptation to lock horns with and thrash Perry. If he could manage to, it would be the first time in years that mentor would wind up in pupil's debt. The possibility excited Horne.

Again seven-card stud. By the drop of the fifth card— Judge Woodward dealing—the last two other players folded, leaving uncle and nephew in the confrontation. Horne had kings wired in the hole; what Perry had there was hard to determine. But he was betting like he had a full house. He showed a pair of sevens. Horne showed no pair, but the third king had fallen to him on the fourth card. He also had one of Perry's sevens, and had seen the case seven turned over when one of the locals folded.

Perry, to be sure, had not missed seeing that; still,

he continued to bet heavily. Two of his three up cards were spades. He could be working on a flush, deduced Horne, but knowing Perry and his style in seven-card stud, he doubted it. More likely he had aces wired in the hole. Had he queens or jacks he would not be betting into the kings. He didn't have to see them to know from Horne's up cards that he had kings wired at the very least in the hole. Meanwhile, neither of the other two aces had appeared; although this was no assurance that they, at least one, hadn't been buried in one of the folder's down cards.

But Perry evidently thought otherwise and continued to bet as if convinced that he would catch one of the other on his sixth, at worst his seventh card. He caught a useless four on the sixth card. What he caught on the seventh was not immediately apparent. Horne caught a three, giving him kings full of threes.

He bet. Perry took an unusually long time deciding what to do. He had already checked his final down card. He looked disconsolate—"gray around the edges," as he would have described another sitting in his place. Horne knew that he knew he was facing three kings. Not having filled his full house, not even having three of a kind, he was in no position to continue playing, but for some unknown reason perhaps vanity, perhaps his petty streak arousing itself, he flung caution and common sense to the winds and attempted a bluff.

Horne couldn't believe his ears. Perry knew what he held, knew he himself couldn't compete. A bluff at this point could only be charitably described as bone-stupid. Horne had checked his king high.

"Three hundred," murmured Perry.

"One thousand," said Horne.

The other players and the kibitzers, including Agatha, caught their breaths in unison. Perry was eyeing him sourly.

"Take it."

The game ended twenty minutes later. Judge Woodward had played well after the debacle involving Horne

and came back to a point where she was close to eight
hundred dollars ahead. The big loser was Perry. After
losing to Horne, he continued to draw good cards. The
worst kind of cards: good enough to stay, not good
enough to win. One after another player would outdraw
him. It slowly took the wind out of his sails, dampened
his spirits, soured his disposition, stirred his bile, and
ignited a flame of resentment in his eyes every time he
looked Horne's way.

The game over, Horne sat counting his money. He
then counted out $450 and handed it to Agatha.

"For services excellently rendered."

Judge Woodward, the other players, and the onlookers had filed out, leaving the three of them. Agatha
thanked Horne.

"I don't have the single I owe you, Perry," he said,
trying his best to keep from sounding triumphant.
"Would you settle for a ten-spot?"

Perry took it without a word.

"What are you going to do now?" Agatha asked
pointedly

"Go to bed."

"And tomorrow?"

"Leave town."

"Going back to Skagway, aren't you?" rasped Perry.

"I don't know."

"Liar."

"Perry . . ." murmured Agatha.

"He's going back, all right, look at his face. You'll
never learn, will you? Go ahead, dive back into the
soup. Botch things up all over again. Only this time you
won't be so lucky; this time you'll wind up in Sitka. My
boy, why must you be so pigheaded? You've got a
hatful of money; take it and go back to the States.
Bank half and run the other half up to ten times as
much. You can do it."

"Will you come back to Skagway with me? I'd very
much appreciate it."

Perry hesitated and glanced at Agatha, giving himself

away. She had her hooks into him, reflected Horne, and he loved it.

"No, thank you," said Perry. He offered her his arm. "Shall we go, my dear? Good night, T.G. We can get together for breakfast in the morning if you like."

"I'd like that if I'm still here."

"We'll stop by the desk, say nine o'clock?" Perry was studying him archly. "You'll either be here or not. On second thought, maybe we'd better play it safe and say our good-byes now."

"Good-bye, Perry . . . Agatha."

Horne smiled and walked out, slipping his fat wad of winnings into his inside jacket pocket.

16

Horne was halfway up the block when Judge Miriam Woodward caught up with him. She took hold of his arm.

"Walk with me."

It sounded like a judicial order. Unwilling to invite a fine for failure to comply, he nodded. She walked him the six blocks home. Her home. By the time they reached the front stoop, tension had begun to take hold in his gut. Agatha was past fifty; Miriam had to be fifty-eight if she was a day. He gathered that she felt he owed her for her letting him off with little more than a slap on the wrist. He felt he owed her. It was the form of payment that they appeared to disagree on. He would have settled for buying her a new shawl. She was, alas, old enough to be his mother. He had never slept with a woman more than ten years older than he. Sleeping with a fifty-eight-year-old threatened disaster. At best it would be excruciatingly inhibiting. If, as he plowed, he could see her face, he would not be able to avoid the impression that he was taking advantage of a grown man's mother.

Somebody was certainly taking advantage!

On the other hand, he supposed he could consider it a form of charity. His contribution wouldn't break him, but being more or less railroaded into giving did not sit comfortably in the back of his mind.

By the time she got him up the stairs and into her tastefully if archaically furnished boudoir, she was panting lustily, baring her teeth, and good-eyeing him with a devouring gleam. She couldn't get their clothes off fast enough. She practically threw him onto the bed.

Naked as a jay, she didn't have a bad body for a woman her years. Her derriere sagged a trifle, and her enormous breasts, suffering from overweight as they did, hung fairly low, but her skin was unwrinkled and she had very good legs. The area of turnoff was her face. She was not viciously homely—in fact, better-looking than Agatha by a long shot—but her baleful glass eye, which seemed to be embedded in the vacated socket purely for the purpose of intimidating anyone who dared look at it, and the bullying expression that clung to her face were not calculated to relax him so he might enjoy himself. But then, he wasn't there to enjoy himself. She was, and it was up to him to provide the enjoyment.

She began massaging his cock gently between her hands, building rigidity into it. Since the moment they entered the house she hadn't uttered a word. She only breathed, loudly, lustfully. He, on the other hand, kept up a running patter.

"Lovely house, lovely stairs, very sturdy. I like mahogany in a house. I like that lamp. Beautiful bedroom. What's that scent, honeysuckle? It is, isn't it? Bed looks very comfortable. Careful, don't tear off that button. My, but your fingers are agile. You must do this oft—I mean. Is it warm in here or is it me? It must be me, I'm sure the temperature's perfect. My, but you have a lovely body for a woman your—I mean. Easy, hey, easy! You're hurting my shoulder. Oh, dear, oh, my, oooo. Ohhhhh! Ahhhhh . . ."

She began giving him head, sucking noisily, enthusiastically, capably. Very. He came in no time. She set about jerking him off, getting it hard again. She seemed in a dreadful hurry. Did edging closer to the grave do that to older women? Possibly. He couldn't be sure, this being his initial experience with one. Impatient with his failure to develop a second erection in thirty seconds, she quit jerking and sucked him hard as a bullet.

She still hadn't said one word. He mounted and penetrated her. She lay like a half-filled sack of barley, not moving a smidgen, except to widen her legs to better engorge his cock. He did all the work. He finally came and was preparing to come again when she squealed, beamed, and climaxed.

"Oooooooooooooo."

Satisfaction overwreathed her face. She licked her lips, closed her eyes, and was asleep. Slowly, carefully, he withdrew and lifted himself off the bed. She was beginning to snore. Carefully, gently, he put on his clothes, covered her with the blanket folded at the foot of the bed, and boots in hand, tiptoed out, easing the door closed behind him.

He made it down the stairs to the foyer, put on his boots, and left. Outside on the sidewalk he paused to light a Jersey cheroot. A window flew open above.

"Thank you. Good night. Stay out of trouble and never pull to an inside straight."

Perry groaned and rolled over in bed. Agatha tittered kittenishly and, taking hold of his shoulder, rolled him back over on his back. She set her hand on his exposed privates, his limp and withered organ and his limp and withered, frightfully wrinkled empty balls. He gazed up at her, his blues eyes more pitiful than piercing, and with a glint of fear in them.

"Let's play some more, dear," she cooed. "Just relax, Mommy will do all the work."

Mommy had been doing most of the work over the course of the last four hours. He lay prone, inert, defenseless against her predatory advances. And let her have her way with him. That she was milking a dry goat did not seem to occur to her. She so refused to believe that her sexual gymnastics had so completely exhausted him that he was beginning to see himself edge closer and closer to death's door. Could a grown man in good health be fucked to death? Absolutely! No question. He was seventy-three years old and was equipped with a seventy-three year old cock. What passed for an erection for him was pathetic, but ostensibly adequate for her needs. The woman was as voracious as a starving vulture. She kept going, kept him going, despite his protestations and pleadings and demands for a respite. She seemed to think that if she stopped, if only for sixty seconds, her heart would stop.

She resumed playing with him.

"It's soft as whipped cream."

"I'm no spring chicken, my dear."

"You're as young as you feel."

"I feel a hundred going on two."

She tittered kittenishly. "You are a caution. Come, come, concentrate, put your heart into it, for pity's sakes. Try . . ."

"Are you going for some sort of record, is that it?"

"Concentrate, Pericles . . ."

He closed his eyes and dispatched his mind a thousand miles from there and fifty years back in time. He pictured himself as he was at twenty-three: young, virile, handsome, strolling down a country lane with a lovely attached to each arm. He had on his Sunday suit and his first wide-brimmed hat. Larks twittered, wildflowers bobbed their colorful heads, a single fluffy, pure white cloud floated overhead. The sky was the blue of his eyes: one of the girls said so, the other agreed.

"Are you concentrating?"

"Mmmm."

"Look! It's starting. Marvelous! I knew you could do it."

He opened one eye hesitantly and peered down his naked length. He could feel no change whatsoever, but evidently he was beginning to get hard. She seemed to think so, for she doubled her stroke and then went down on him, gobbling him greedily, punishing his head brutally, buffeting it about inside her cavernous mouth with her tongue. No slave in history was ever so cruelly, so mercilessly thrashed. She got him bow-hard, the only description that would apply. Not a railroad-spike, not even wooden-dowel hard, but fairly, flexibly stiff, like an archer's willow bow, bending easily, holding its shape all too briefly. Knowing it was "make it fast or you're out of luck," she jerked her mouth free, mounted him swiftly, and plugged him into her quim. She began bouncing lightly, sparing his thighs her weight, driving up and down, up and down.

"How does it feel, dear?"

"Mmmmm."

"It feels wonderful. It does, really. I mean I can feel it."

"Mmmmmm."

Her bouncing, now comingling with gyrating, grew more vigorous. To Perry she looked as if she were cantering a horse.

"I'm coming, I'm coming, I'm coming, I'm coming . . ."

Up, around, and down; up, around, and down. Now she was slamming down violently, not sparing his hip-bones at all. What if she fractured them? he thought. He envisioned himself hobbling along on two canes, reaching his wheelchair, sinking into it. Up, around, and down; up, around, and down.

"Coming, coming, coming, coming, ooooooooo."

She stopped abruptly and smiled down, her eyes glazed, her panting subsided, segueing into gentle, contented breathing.

"That was marvelous. You were wonderful. Did you come?"

"I have no idea."

"Want me to make you?"

"It's not important, Agatha. As long as you're satisfied."

"I am, I am. It was wonderful. You're a masterful lover, Pericles."

His eyes snapped wide. "I am?"

"I adore you making love to me. Feeling your strength, your virility, manliness. You make me feel like putty in your hands."

She had dismounted. Again her hand crept to his privates and began gently stroking. His hand shot out covering hers.

"Give it a few minutes, dear. There's no rush."

"Nonsense, don't be such an old stick. Just relax, leave everything to Mommy. Take a deep breath, let it out slowly, and concentrate, concentrate . . ."

Horne returned to the hotel and went to bed, but despite his abrupt return to affluence and the salutary effect it had on his nerves, he could not fall asleep. The more he thought about returning to Skagway, the more problems presented themselves, the dicier it looked. He would have to buy a gun; he couldn't go back into battle unarmed. He'd have to steer clear of Deputy Marshal Meriweather, if that was possible in such a small town. He'd have to plan his every move from the time he set foot on the dock with the utmost care and attention to detail. Even if he did, he could hardly plan for those things he'd have no control over and could not anticipate. Perry was right: the first time around he shouldn't have gone off half-cocked, barging into the store and confronting Louis. Thinking back on it now, now that he felt so much better about life, no longer sorry for himself, demoralized and defeated, he had only gotten what he'd deserved; his rashness had earned him the safe door to the head.

Lucian and Louis. One had smacked him in the back of the head, the other in the side. Perhaps he should invest in a medieval helmet. A gun, definitely; also a satchel of some kind to carry the money when he recovered it. How to go about that was the problem. From which brother, also a problem. He had no way of knowing if Lucien was still carrying such a sum; Louis certainly had it. Anyone less ethical than he would not make a distinction between them: take the money from

Louis, let him square things with Lucien. They were a team, they helped each other. Better Lucien be in Louis' debt that his. What if it came to that? Came to his having no choice but to take from Louis what Lucien owed him? Before it reached that pass he'd have to get hold of Lucien, get him someplace alone and make him pay. At least try.

He thought about Marion. When the four of them had walked by him sitting on the bench, she'd had her arm slipped through Louis', making a show of affection, even though she felt none. Had she done that for his benefit? Could be. John Meriweather had told him of the rumor that she had a thing for Lucien; displaying her feelings for her husband in Lucien's presence did seem to weaken that possibility.

"Who the hell knows?"

On the other hand, if she did have eyes for Lucien, it was possible—although he couldn't figure how at the moment—he might be able to exploit it to his advantage. But the overall problem remained: he knew very little about any of them; he'd be operating in their backyard, at the same time doing his best to keep out of Meriweather's way. What would the deputy do if he ran into him? He couldn't arrest him; on what charge? He'd most likely order him to leave town, see him to the dock and onto a southbound ship. He was within his rights to chase him—had a duty to, actually.

He washed, shaved, dressed, and went downstairs to pay his bill. It was about a quarter-to-nine. He thought about hanging around until nine to see if Perry and Agatha showed up, but then thought better of it. He didn't need another discussion with Perry; it would only degenerate into argument and they'd part with ill feelings, which would be embarrassing for Agatha. What, he wondered, was Perry up to with her? He seemed to be glued to her. Was he smitten? Was he so lonely he'd persuaded himself he was in love? Did he intend to propose?

"My God!"

The desk clerk looked up as she handed him his change.

"Nothing," he mumbled, "talking to myself."

He stopped at a gun shop and bought an ancient Colt .45; three dollars' worth of self-defense for ten dollars. If anything, Juneau's prices were even more outrageous than Skagway's. 'Twas ever thus in gold country. Next door to the gun shop he bought a new alligator bag, a near duplicate of Perry's. It would serve to carry the sixty thousand when he recovered it from Lucien.

He had breakfast at the hotel, then walked to the docks. Despite having had less than four hours' sleep, he felt rested and in good spirits. The daily mail packet left for Skagway at one o'clock. It was a three-hour trip. His ticket cost him seventeen dollars.

With nearly three hours to kill, he took another walk around town, hoping he wouldn't bump into Perry and Agatha. The Governor's Mansion at the corner of Ninth Street and Calhoun Avenue looked vacant. Its colonial-style architecture, the tall, smooth, bone-white supporting pillars on the porch contrasted with nearby Indian totem poles. He lingered on the banks of Gold Creek, watching the wild birds for a time, then made his way up Willoughby and down to the waterfront.

The sixty miles to Skagway would have been boring were it not for the spectacular scenery. He stood at the rail all the way up the Lynn Canal. They passed only one southbound vessel, the *Klondike Princess*. Sight of Skagway nestled at the base of the glacier quickened his heart. He resolved to stick to the outskirts of town until dark before starting on his quest. That way there'd be less chance of his bumping into Meriweather. He really should avoid him at all costs; if they did meet, any excuse he fabricated for coming back would be unacceptable. He envisioned the deputy marshal grabbing his collar and bum's-rushing him back down to the docks, insisting as he did so that it was for his protection.

He hung around the dock until it grew dark. Skagway came alive with lights and the drunken, boisterous evening traffic. Businesses closed for the day, save for the saloons, gambling halls, and dance halls. At eight-thirty, the night having become as dark as it would get, he made his way in roundabout fashion to Ninth Avenue, going up Alaska Street paralleling the Skagway River on the west side of town, turning into Ninth, crossing Main, and approaching the store.

Slender rods of light showed at the sides of the drawn shades at the front. He approached the door; it was locked. He nevertheless got the feeling that the lights were not night-lights. There was someone inside— probably Louis—although try as he might, he could not get the proper angle, peering in past the edge of one shade after another, to get a good-enough look at the office area.

He checked his newly purchased gun, making sure it was fully loaded, and ventured down the side alley. A flight of stairs ascended to the second floor. He climbed up to a door. No light showed from within. He tried the door and to his surprise found it unlocked. In he went.

He blinked in the darkness of a small room, quite like a doctor's waiting room. Moonlight defined a couple of chairs and a low table and the door to the second-floor storage area. He went inside. There were dozens of crates, all quite large, some gaping open, most securely nailed. Among those that were open some were empty, three half-filled with pelts. At the far end pale light glowed around the top of the stairs.

Gun in hand, he made his way through the crates to it. Shoving his gun into his belt, clutching the satchel in one hand, he started down the stairs, moving slowly, stealthily. Reaching the bottom, he looked about. Four lamps burned, brightly illuminating the office.

The safe was wide open. It was empty. He heard steps. He reached for his gun. John Meriweather showed himself from behind a bearskin hanging from its holder. He leveled his weapon.

"Give it here, T.G."

Horne hesitated.

Meriweather came striding toward him. He jerked the gun from his grasp. "What the hell are you doing here?" he rasped. "Need I ask?" He nodded at the satchel in his hand. "I'm afraid you're a little late."

"What the devil happened?"

"Fireworks. About two hours ago. Louis was working late, catching up on business he'd let slide going down to Juneau, I guess. Intruder murdered him. The people across the street heard three shots and sent a boy for me. When I got here, the front door was wide open, the safe as you see it. He was lying on the floor with two bullets in his chest, one in his head."

"If you think—"

"Take it easy, nobody's accusing you." He sniffed the muzzle of Horne's gun. "This thing hasn't been fired. I'll give you one guess who did it."

"His wife."

He smiled grimly. "She was spotted leaving lugging a carpetbag that turned out to be filled with the contents of the safe. Trapper contracts, canceled checks, everything. I caught up with her back at their place. She was planning to leave on the eight-o'clock packet for Anchorage."

"North?"

"Northwest."

"My God. Where was Lucien while all this was going on?"

"I already checked on him. He was seen leaving on a southbound ship earlier today, the *Klondike Princess*."

"The Klon . . . the ship I came up on passed it on the way. He was on board. Goddammit to hell!"

"Heading back to the States."

"The bastard! The son of a bitch!"

"That was pretty much Marion's opinion. He evidently doublecrossed her. From the little I could gather when I locked her up, he was supposed to take off for Anchorage with her."

"She told you that?"

"In so many words. She put on quite a show. Wasn't

the least bit afraid, not ashamed of murdering Louis, not sorry. Kept calling him a monster, brute, tyrant. Not exactly the Louis everybody in Skagway knew, including yours truly. But who knows what goes on in any marraige behind closed doors? You should have heard her brag about how crazy Lucien was about her, spouting off about how they'd be together forever, claiming he couldn't live without her."

"He's taking a stab at it."

"Then I told her about his heading south. She went wild; I thought she'd claw my face off."

"Where was her father while all this was going on?"

"Who knows? He might not even have come back from Juneau."

"What did you do with Louis?"

"His body was taken over to Ormsby's on Spring Street. Just up from Second Avenue near the harbor. Why?"

Horne shrugged. "Just wondered."

"He wasn't wearing your stickpin and watch if that's what you're thinking."

"Could they have been in the carpetbag with the contents of the safe?"

"I can't say. I haven't had a chance to examine it. Soon as I got word that she'd been seen leaving here after the shots were fired, I went to her house, arrested her, brought her to jail. Then came here." He pointed to a spot on the floor. "Found Louis lying there where the blood is, the safe open as you see it, the lights on. I was just taking a last look around when you came down the stairs."

"The *Klondike Princess*. You wouldn't happen to know where it's heading, would you?"

"Somebody should know down at the docks."

"The bastard's got a good six-hour head start on me."

"Better. There won't be any southbound boats leaving here until tomorrow morning. I'm sorry, T.G., but I am relieved that you'll be taking your problem with him out of my yard. I've already got my hands full with this murder. So the rumor turned out right, after all; she was cheating on Louis with Lucien."

"He played along with her, had a good time, she kills Louis to clear the way for them, and he runs out on her. Talk about just desserts."

"The little I've been able to talk to her, I think she's gone off her rocker. She'll end up in a mental hospital, not prison. By the way, did you want to see her for anything?"

"No, thanks. I would like to get a look at what's inside the bag, though."

"It won't do you any good. If you did find your things, I wouldn't be able to give them to you. Like Judge Woodward said, they're legally Louis'."

"He's got no use for them now."

"So they're part of his estate."

"Murderers can't inherit."

"All the same, there is an estate, and everything in it—the business, the merchandise, and your watch and stickpin—is included. If Lucien didn't reclaim them. He probably did."

"Of course he did."

Meriweather handed his gun back. "The rest of your arsenal's back at the office. You can pick it up anytime."

"Tomorrow morning'll do."

"Be careful with that thing, will you? At least while you're in town."

"How can I be otherwise? My bird's flown."

"That could be lucky." Horne accorded him a look that questioned his mentality. "You chase him, catch up with him in the States out of Judge Woodward's bailiwick, out from under that two-year suspended sentence and you'll have a clear field."

"*If* I catch up with him."

"Oh, you will. In Portland or Patagonia, someplace. You won't quit till you do. To come back to Skagway after what you were put through here, not to mention down in Juneau, brother, you're one of a kind. You never let go."

"Would you?"

"I don't know, only some things can turn out more trouble than they're worth trying to put to right. Even when it is 'the principle of the thing.' You got a place to stay?"

"I'll go over and sign back into the Golden North. Don't worry, I can afford it. That reminds me, I owe you." He handed him a dollar and a half. "For Doc Shaker's visit. Also, here's your twenty. It was very generous of you, John." Meriweather looked properly puzzled. "Come on, don't pretend you didn't slip that twenty into my pocket. That was half a month's salary."

"Only a third. I felt sorry for you. I've never seen anyone look so down and out. Besides, I sort of let you down on the witness stand."

"You're a very special guy, you know that?"

"Yeah. Don't forget to pick up your hardware and knuckle-duster tomorrow. If I'm not in, I'll tell whoever is to expect you. Your stuff'll be in the bottom drawer."

"Thank you, John."

"Good luck, T.G. Good hunting." He paused. "Seriously, how long do you intend to give it?"

"Just until I catch him."

"Why do I bother to ask?"

They shook hands and parted at the front door.

17

Next morning Horne set out for the jail. Upon arriving, he took pains not to go near the cell area; he didn't want to be seen by or see Marion. Standing near the inner door talking to one of Meriweather's assistants, he heard her cat meow. While the assistant was digging out his guns, he got a good look at the contents of the carpetbag dumped out on a table—everything he'd seen earlier in the safe, except his Jürgensen. There was the strongbox—still packed with money, he imagined.

From the jail he went directly to Ormsby's Funeral Parlor. He talked to the owner and confirmed Meriweather's assertion that Louis' body was brought in with neither stickpin nor watch.

His third stop was down at the docks where he spoke with the dock master. He was told that the *Klondike Princess* would have made the usual stops on the way down to her destination, Seattle. Lucien would not tarry there, he knew. On the run as he was with better than half a day's lead, he might very well keep going for another month. This thought, of course, didn't discourage T.G. from following; he'd followed others clear across the country by the simple expedient of connecting one leg to the next. When Lucien got to Seattle he'd probably take a train south or east. Horne need only ask at the station.

One thing he could be sure of: unlike on the trek

from Hurdlesford, his quarry would not be entering his final destination in any hotel register. Also, he'd be deliberately trying to throw him off his track, bribing ticket agents and others to misdirect him.

But if it took him ten years to catch up, so be it. The dock master checked the daily sailing schedule. The next boat taking passengers heading down the Lynn Canal was the *Henrietta Blandings*, a packet due to leave in an hour and a half.

T.G. went back to the hotel to collect his things and check out. He was preparing to leave the room, taking a last look around to make sure he hadn't forgotten anything, when a timid knock sounded.

It was Mr. King. He had trimmed his mustache by a third since Horne last saw it in Juneau; he appeared exhausted, as if the sudden rush of recent dire events had completely overwhelmed him. He looked shrunken; he apologized for coming.

"But I had to speak with you." He noticed the bag on the bed. "You're leaving. Of course, you would be. It's about my daughter."

"Come on."

He sat twirling the curled brim of his fedora nervously between his fingers. He was a pitiable sight; Horne felt extremely sorry for him. Things had happened over which he had no control, but this did not lessen the severity of their impact.

"She's been arrested for murdering her husband."

"I heard."

"I've just come from the jail. She's in a frightful state, barely coherent, carrying on like a madwoman. It's all like a horrible nightmare. Do you remember back when they put us off the *Charles E. Sterling?* We were sitting in the rear of the dory. She had a gun . . ."

"She tried to shoot me."

"I pushed her arm. I . . . saved your life."

"You did."

"I've come to ask a favor of you. Quid pro quo. You do owe me."

"What do you want, Mr. King?"

"You to alibi for her. Tell them you were with her last night when Louis was killed. You were . . . here at the hotel or at her place, anywhere . . ."

"That's impossible. Even if I agreed to, nobody'd believe me. Witnesses heard the shots, saw her leaving the front way carrying a bag filled with the contents—"

"I know, I know, but they could be lying, or imagined it was her they saw. It was dark. But if you testified you were with her it'd be your word against theirs."

"I'm sorry."

"But you must! You're my only hope. They can't find her guilty, she can't go to prison."

"From what I've heard she won't."

King brightened, his eyes lighting up. Horne had inadvertently given him hope, which wasn't at all his intention. All he wanted to do was straighten out his thinking.

"I have to tell you that there are those who think she's gone off the deep end. Shooting her husband pushed her off."

"She's crazy? That's absurd! Preposterous! Her mother, yes, poor suffering woman. That I'll admit, but not Marion. She's as sane as you or I. Please, I'm begging you, testify in her behalf. You must, you're our only hope."

"It wouldn't do any good."

"I'll give you five thousand dollars, ten thousand—"

"I don't want your money. Try to think about it rationally; before she even comes to trial, she's sure to be examined by an alienist."

"She's not crazy!"

"Ssssh, please . . ."

"She's not. I know my daughter, I tell you."

"And you love her."

"Adore her! She's the air I breathe."

"Then, for God's sakes stand by her. Do what's best for her, don't try to manipulate things. Let her be examined; they'll determine her mental state. If she needs it she'll be given proper treatment, she'll be helped."

"They'll stick her away in some bedlam just as they did Cora. They can't do that to my little girl, they won't. For the last time, will you help?"

"I'm sorry, Mr. King."

He jumped up, flinging his arms, his face reddening, jowls quivering. "Ungrateful wretch! Heartless villain!"

Out he stormed, slamming the door.

It was the day before, back in Juneau, the time shortly before Horne boarded his boat to Skagway. Perry got quietly up from the bed, leaving Agatha snoring. He went into the bathroom and studied his image in the mirror. He looked frightful: pale, haggard, his eyes dull, their usual sparkle entirely absent. He felt as if he'd been pulled through a wringer. His legs shook and he had to grip the washbasin to hold himself upright. For a moment he imagined that his leg bones and joints had dissolved, leaving only the skin to support him. Gradually, he steadied himself, pulled down one eye, then the other, groaning with each, then examined his tongue. It was so coated it looked to be frosted. He glanced back at the sleeper, his suspicions conformed: she was slowly killing him.

He cast about in sudden desperation. He had to get out once. He stealthily and speedily packed his bag. Not daring to close the clasps for fear of awakening her, he dropped it out the window into the petunias, then dressed, feeling like a bondservant, a slave plotting escape. The definition fit. What was he but a prisoner of her lust? She couldn't get enough of him; she'd gotten virtually all there was! One more go-round would surely be the death of him while, ironically, scarcely even tiring her. She had the stamina of a bull elephant and was insatiable; three men a third his age wouldn't have satisfied her.

His hand drifted toward his fly and his suffering

privates; he hesitated to touch them for fear they'd drop off. He would be months recovering.

He went back into the bathroom. He was seventy-two going on ninety. Every night in her bed, five in all so far, had pushed him two years closer to the grave. He was literally fleeing for his life.

He put his hat on. She stopped snoring, rolled over, licked her lips noisily, and one-eyed him, while her artificial eyes stared from its glass on the night table.

"Dear heart," she mumbled sleepily.

"Agatha, my love. Did you sleep well?"

"Log . . . Come here, I want you." Her eye was fully open now. She saw that he was dressed. "What are you doing? Where are you going?"

"Just out for some cigars. Be back in fifteen minutes."

"Do hurry." She writhed sensuously under the sheet. "I'll be waiting. Come kiss me good-bye."

She had a heart of pure gold, she was brilliant, she adored him; despite her voracious appetite for him, she was gentle. He liked her, possibly even loved her. But the possibility of dying in the act was all too frightening.

He kissed her and went out. Outside he walked around the little house to the backyard, retrieved his bag, and headed for the docks as fast as he could walk. Thoughts of T.G. came flocking to mind. Damn him! Damn and double damn his arrant obstinacy, running back to Skagway. He would not follow him; never again would he venture to within fifty miles of that terrible place. He loathed and despised it beyond all reason, chiefly because it scared him so.

But he had to get out of Juneau—catch the first boat out of Alaska and never come back.

T.G. had nearly cleaned him out in the game the night before. Deliberately, he was certain. He'd left him with less than two hundred dollars, the poorest he'd been in ages. It was enough to get him back to the States, however. He'd hunt up a game in Seattle or Portland, wherever the boat wound up, rebuild his treasury at the expense of the locals, and set out for San

Antonio. If T.G. got out of Skagway alive without getting into trouble a second time, if he had the brains of a toad, he'd head for San Antonio himself.

On further thought Perry didn't greatly care whether he did or not. The boy was putting undue pressure on their friendship lately, taking a lot for granted: demanding favors left and right, borrowing money practically every other day, arguing with him at every turn.

What did he need with such aggravation in these, his twilight years? He needed serenity, peace of mind, loyalty, and a kind word. Let T.G. catch up with him. Better he get the Frenchman out of his system and out of his life.

Arriving at the docks he was told that a packet from Skagway would be stopping off in about twenty minutes. He would have preferred five minutes. He glanced warily back toward town and wondered if Agatha was beginning to get restless. He'd told her he'd be back in fifteen minutes. It was already at least that. When it got to be twenty, she'd get up, get dressed, and come looking for him. Once out of the house she'd head straight for the docks.

"Twenty minutes did you say?" he asked his informant.

"Twenty or thirty. Packet could be late, most always is a little."

Perry sighed, thanked him, walked off, and hid behind the largest crate on the wharf.

18

Both Skagway and Juneau together could have fit into one corner of Seattle. The dock area alone looked to be two miles long. Boasting ten times Skagway's and Juneau's combined square miles and three times their population, Seattle squatted on a neck of land between Elliott Bay and the freshwater Lake Washington, about 865 miles by water north of San Francisco. It was the terminus of the Northern Pacific and the Great Northern railroads, and its setting was magnificent.

When the *Henrietta Blandings* put in and Horne debarked, he resolved to head straight for the railroad station in hopes of finding a ticket agent who recognized Lucien DeBlois. He had not walked ten paces from the gangplank before a familiar voice called his name.

Sauntering up came Perry, tugging on a stogie and all smiles. Horne's astonishment at the sight of him broadened his smile.

"Surprise, surprise."

"What the devil—"

"No pun intended, I take it you missed your boat up in Skagway."

"So I was late."

Perry leered. "Hold on to your hat, my boy. Better lean against this pile of crates, this might prove too much for your ticker. Guess who my traveling compan-

158

ion down from Juneau was." He nodded. "In the flesh, complete with your stickpin and watch. He even gave me the time when I asked him."

"He recognized you."

Perry took him by the arm and walked them toward the street. "You're not thinking. How could he, he's never seen me."

"In Hurdlesford—"

"He'd already left by the time I got there. We never did turn him up in Skagway, not while I was with you. He didn't come to the trial. He wouldn't know me if he fell over me. He practically did strolling about the deck of the *Klondike Princess*."

"What made you take the same boat?"

"I was under a bit of pressure to get out of town. It happened to be the first boat by. To be perfectly candid, I decided it was in the best interests of my health to flee Agatha Trent Woodward."

"You had a fight?"

"Perish forbid. Once firmly established in the lady's affections, she turned out to be as peaceful as an angel. Never a harsh word between us. The problem was she had her eye on the altar, and you know how even casual talk about marriage distresses me, frightens me."

"Why don't you tell the truth. She was too much for you to handle."

"Balderdash! If anything it was the other way around."

"Did she ever say what happened between her and her sister?"

"Both had their eye on the same beau aeons ago. Reading between the lines, I gather he took advantage and played one off against the other, then left town with a third girl. To this day each blames the other for souring him on her. Not what you'd call a fresh plot. Alas, some men can be viciously painful. Speaking of which, your quarry is registered at the Washington Plaza. Fifth and Westlake. I followed him there, saw him go in and register."

"He's staying here in Seattle?"

"At least for the night. I expect you could inquire at the desk as to how long he intends to stay."

"Not long. He probably just wants to relax and rest up before staring on his long journey."

"You still think he's worried you'll catch up with him?"

"You bet he is."

They walked toward the center of town and the Washington Plaza Hotel. Horne filled Perry in on the melodramatic events in Skagway.

"John Meriweather thinks she's crazy. If she wasn't when she shot Louis, she could have cracked when she found out Lucien had walked out on her."

"Maybe he suspected she already was, and that's why we left."

"I don't know about that; my guess is he never intended to take her with him. Used her, abused her, and dropped her. One thing puzzles me, though; why didn't he wait till after she cleaned out the safe? The last time I saw it, Louis' strongbox was crammed with cash. Of course, Lucien already had mine. Maybe he figured passing up the money was a fair price to pay for getting away from her."

"At the risk of repeating myself, in all that's transpired between your arrest and your arrival here, have you had time to figure out how you're going to handle him when you do catch up? Better than you handled Louis, I would hope."

"I made a mistake. Didn't you ever?"

"Not that I recall. I had a thought if you're interested." Horne's failure to say anything indicated he was. "Walk up to him, give him your biggest, friendliest hello, act like nothing happened. Better yet, tell him you're willing to let bygones be bygones, get into a game with him, and beat the pants off him."

"Win back what he stole from me . . ."

"Why not?"

"Why should I have to? Win what already belongs to

me? I wouldn't call that bending over backward. I call it asinine."

"You want your money, don't you? What else can you do? Climb through his window in the dead of night and whack him over the head?"

"It's what he deserves."

"Be sensible, T.G. Put some thought into the thing before you go on the attack. Use your head for a change instead of your famous hair-trigger temper. If you think about it, you're no better off now than you were the day we landed in Skagway. Oh, you know where to find him and you won't confuse him with Louis—nobody'll ever do that again—but you have no way of knowing he's got your money."

"Of course he has. You don't think he buried it under a rock up there, do you?"

"Let's think about it, please?"

"I already have; I've thought it to death. When we get to the hotel I'm going straight up to his room and have it out. What the hell, he knows I'm chasing him. Knows why—"

"And what if he doesn't come across?"

"He'll have to."

"Or you'll shoot him."

"I may just do that."

"Of course." Perry threw up his hands. "You'll never change. There's just no getting through that concrete skull. Very well, do as you please, just don't ask me to back you up, shill for you, work on him . . ."

"All I'm asking you to do is show me where the damned hotel is!"

Perry waited in the lobby, appropriating a chair so large he looked like a boy sitting in it. He had started another cigar and was puffing vigorously on it, seething in annoyance, watching T.G. out of the corner of his eye through a curtain of smoke as he approached the desk.

Monsieur Lucien DeBlois was registered, Monsieur Lucien DeBlois was in.

"Room Four B."

Horne ascended the stairs two at a time, striding resolutely down the hall, pausing before the door, checking his .45, and knocking. Lucien came to the door at once. He was in his shirtsleeves, his jacket on a hanger suspended from the top drawer pull of the bureau, his suitcase open on the bed. He smiled graciously.

"Monsieur Reechardson, what a pleasant surprise!"

"I'll bet."

"Come een, come een, of all people . . ."

"Let's start off right, shall we? Without the bullshit."

"Bool . . . ?"

"I want my money, sixty thousand and forty dollars. To the penny."

Lucien's face fell. "I do not understand."

"You climbed the ladder, knocked me over the head, stole it. What am I telling you what you already know for? Oh, it was you, I didn't even have to see you, your stinking orange blossoms gave you away."

"Orange ... what een zee worl' are you talkeeng about? As God ees my weetness . . ."

Horne cut him off with a wave and drew his gun. "Just hand it over and I'll be out of here."

"Seexty thousand and forty dollars you say? An extraordeenary amount. I have not seen such a sum een ages. I have about seventy dollars; eef you weesh, feel free to search my belongeengs. Go over zee entire room."

"You obviously wouldn't keep that kind of money here. It's down in the hotel safe along with my pin and watch."

"*Mon ami*, you seem to know everytheeng about me. You are perhaps zee clairvoyant?"

"Let's go."

"As you weesh, but you are wasteeng your time. I have only zee seventy dollar."

"Listen to me, you lying son of a bitch, I've had you

up to here! I've been choking on you since Hurdlesford.
Up in Skagway, Juneau, all over the landscape. I want
my goddamn money!"

He cocked and brandished the gun. Lucien did not
react in fear; instead, he sighed, smiled benignly, shook
his head, and brashly turned his back on him.

"Let me tell you what really happen; you are entitled to know. I confess you are right, eet was I who rob
you; eet ees useless to deny eet. Me and my fatal
attraction for orange blossoms, *nez-pas?* I left Hurdlesford. By zee time I get to Skagway I have lose almost all
zee money on trains and on zee boat up from San
Francisco. A streak of meeserable luck; you are a gambler, I do not have to tell you how luck can turn. By
zee time I get to Skagway I was down to a few hundred.

"Zat ees what happen, zat ees zee truth. You can
believe me or not, eet ees up to you. As for your
steeckpeen and watch, you have no claim to either. You
heard what zee judge say. I purchase zem both legally."

"With my money."

"Ah, zere you have a point."

"Where are they?"

"Gone."

"You were wearing them on the boat coming down."

"Ah, you have zee spy workeeng for you. Yes, I wore
zem; being zee rightful owner, why shouldn't I? Only
two day before we land here, I lose both in a game.
Heart flush to a full house. Meeserable luck."

"You lie! You never stop!"

"*Sacrebleu! Incroyable!* You are like talkeeng to stone;
to you every word out of my mouth ees a lie. I am
eencapable of telling zee truth. Face eet, *mon ami*, we
are at what you call a Mexican standoff, *nez-pas?* Perhaps you had better shoot me after all; only try not to
make too beeg a mess."

Horne had moved to the bed to poke through the
contents of the suitcase with his free hand. He then
checked the bureau drawers. Lucien watched wordlessly,
smiling. Horne finished and glanced about glowering.

"Sateesfied?"

"Downstairs."

"As you weesh."

Horne saw Perry sitting where he'd left him. He turned to watch the proceedings at the hotel safe, his chin barely coming up over the arm of his chair. There were only two envelopes in the safe. One belonged to a woman guest and contained a quantity of antique jewelry; the other was filled with stock and bond certificates being held for a Mr. and Mrs. Crawford. There was also a slim, expensive-looking, engraved box containing a collection of gold coins. That was all.

"Back upstairs," said Horne, consciously increasing the menace in his tone, having been obliged to put his gun way when they came down.

"As you weesh. Only, to what purpose? I have notheeng to geeve you. Eef you want my last seventy dollars, you are welcome to eet."

"Move."

Under Horne's direction Lucien went over every inch of surface in the room as painstakingly as a physician studying specimens on slides under a microscope. Then Horne took an additional hour to examine his clothing; going through his pockets, linings, checking for custom-tailored places of concealment. Three hours passed with no results.

"Sateesfied?" asked Lucien.

"Stop saying that word—I'm sick of hearing it—and I'm not. You've got the money, you've got my things."

"Where?"

"You've got 'em and I'm going to get 'em; I'm going to hound you. I'm going to be walking inside your shoes from now till doomsday if I have to, but . . ."

"Yes?"

"I forgot to tell you. You don't know, there's no way you could, leaving Skagway when you did. I'm afraid I have some bad news, Lucien. Your brother's dead."

Lucien stiffened, then slowly relaxed and softened

his expression into the semblance of a smile. He waggled a finger reprovingly.

"Shame on you, *mon ami*; zat is too far beneath you. You are frustrated, resentful; like zee small boy you want to flail away, inflict pain een retaliation."

"Marion murdered him."

"*Mais non!* Ees not possible!"

"Walked into the store and shot him, one in the head, two in the chest. She brought a large bag with her, planning to clean out the safe. He no doubt objected; she probably didn't go barging in, intending to kill him, but when he refused to cooperate . . . Meriweather's got her locked up. When he showed up at the house to arrest her, he found her packing to leave for Anchorage. To join you."

His words were no longer registering. The realization that he was speaking the truth took hold of his listener. He sank slowly down onto the bed. He looked to be gradually turning gray and was as stiff as stone, paralyzed in shock. Horne stopped talking. Lucien stared at the wall, Horne stared at him.

"Louis," Lucien mumbled.

"I'm not telling you to gloat about it, not talking out of frustration. Meriweather thinks she snapped. Went berserk when Louis turned her down, tried to stop her looting the safe, whatever happened."

"The beetch, the murdering beetch. What weel zey do to her do you theenk?"

"Probably declare her incompetent to stand trial. Put her way in an institution."

"She weel not be puneeshed? But she murdered heem!"

"In the eyes of the law she's not responsible."

"*Incroyable!*"

"I'm no lawyer, I don't know what'll happen."

"I know what should, what I weesh would. Zat I could get her beautiful neck between zees two hands . . ."

Horne continued to study him. He was now holding his head between his hands, shaking it slowly, patently unable to accept what had happened. The way he sat, the way he held himself, slightly cringing, bracing himself, it was as if an invisible spear had been thrust into him and immediately pulled out again. And through sheer force of will he was holding back the outrush of blood.

"Louis, Louis . . ."

Horne took a last, useless look around the room. He thought briefly about the seventy dollars, decided that it was too paltry a sum to even serve as a token payment, and left.

19

Horne shared Perry's room at the Washington Plaza that night. Frustration had taken a firm grip on him; so tenacious was its hold it caused him to lie awake most of the night. He was bleary-eyed and yawning at breakfast the next morning. By contrast, Perry was as fresh as the new day, from all appearances completely recovered from his ordeal with Agatha. They sat at breakfast, Perry attacking his second helping of bacon and eggs. Horne pushed a yolk about aimlessly.

"Back up, T.G., so you've lost. You've lost before. Accept it and go on from here. Face up to it, my boy, nobody can get blood out of a stone."

"He's got everything cached someplace. I know it. I feel it."

"Only because you want to, not because it's so. Give it up, he's broke. He certainly had ample time to lose it all."

"You saw him on board. You mentioned he gave you the time with my watch."

"He did."

"Was he wearing it and the pin when he got off? Think about it before you answer."

"I don't have to."

"Was he or wasn't he?"

"I don't know. I didn't notice, okay? I saw them when I boarded at Juneau, when he gave me the time

167

about an hour later. After that I didn't look for them. I guess because I knew they weren't going anywhere. When we got off in Seattle I was behind him. I stayed behind and followed him to the hotel. I stood outside the door and watched him register, his back to me."

"He turned and went upstairs . . ."

"I don't know if he was wearing them; it didn't register, I tell you."

"You're a big help."

Perry bristled. "I like that! I damn well have been 'a big help.' I tracked him down for you, didn't I? Kept an eye on him. It's not my fault he's tapped out. Are you going to grouse and mewl and pule for the next six years. Why don't you shrug it off, chalk it up to losses, and forget about it?"

"It just doesn't make sense."

"I won't ask what, you'll tell me anyway."

"I know him—how he operates, how he thinks. He's like all gamblers: he has to have it on him, at least within reach, at all times. He brought it down here. He must have. He did!"

"Quiet down, for pity's sakes."

"On the way over from the docks, did he stop off anywhere?"

"He never broke stride, came straight to the hotel."

"When you went back to the docks and met me, he could have skinned out with it, stashed it elsewhere."

"Why can't you believe it's gone? That he lost it playing?"

"He didn't. You should have been in the room with him, seen his face, the way he acted. He was playing with me; he was. Right up when I told him about Louis. That practically knocked him out. But up until then, it was cat-and-mouse with me the mouse. I especially remember when I demanded he turn out his pockets. The smug look on his face."

"What did he have in them?"

"Nothing, not even a kitchen match. Just his room keys. You know what the whole trouble is, he knew I'd be following him, I wouldn't quit till I caught up. He had time to prepare to bamboozle me—"

"What did you just say?" Perry had stopped eating. His expression was almost fearful.

"About what?"

"You said keys; with an 's.'"

"So?"

"Keys, T.G. What was he doing with two? He was by himself. Hotels don't give two keys to single occupants. Only when two people share a room."

"My God! You're absolutely right! He signed for two rooms."

"Occupied one and used the other to stash the money and your things. Knowing you were on his tail, knowing you'd show up."

"Deliberately staying here in Seattle instead of continuing to run. Stopping the chase here so we could have our showdown. He could feed me his sob story, hoping I'd give it up and walk away. Two rooms. Come on, we're going back to the hotel."

"I haven't finished my breakfast."

"Yes you have. Come on!"

The desk clerk on duty was not the clerk Perry had seen the day before when Lucien registered.

"Herbert Arbuckle was on," explained the clerk, a pretty young thing with long, attractive blond hair who seemed to be having a difficult time keeping her eyes off Horne.

He had finished checking the register. L. DeBlois had signed for 4B. No evidence whatever of a second room. He had also, according to the clerk, checked out. No surprise to either Horne or Perry.

"When does Herbert come on today?" Perry asked.

"Noon. He's back in the office. Shall I get him for you?"

"Can we talk in the office?" Horne asked. "In privacy. We'll only be a minute."

She smiled demurely. "I suppose . . ."

She motioned them down to the end of the counter and lifted the board. The office was filled with files and a rolltop desk. A slender boy with a girlish complexion sat reading the *Police Gazette*, his profile to them. He breathed wetly through his prominent and imperfect nose.

"Herbert?" asked Perry.

"Herbert," said Horne impatiently. "We're with the U.S. Secret Service. We're looking for a man, a guest. He uses a number of aliases; he signed the register as L. DeBlois. You signed him in. Four B." Horne described Lucien.

"So?" Herbert snuffled disgustingly, his watery eyes shifting back and forth between them.

"You gave him Four B. You also gave him another room, only you didn't record it. He slipped you something in exchange for one of the holdout rooms, right?"

"You guys really Secret Servicemen? Let's see some kinda identification, okay. I'm not sayin' nothin' to nobody till I see you're for real."

Perry had taken a chair close to the desk. "That's very shrewd, Herbert. You should be suspicious. Let's start again, okay?" He got his money out of his wallet and licking his thumb, laid a ten-dollar bill on the desk alongside Herbert's elbow. Then a second one beside it. Then a third. The boy's eyes sparkled greedily.

"Promise you won't tell Old Man Swales, the manager? I'll get in terrible trouble if he finds out."

"We won't tell a soul," said Horne.

"Swear on your honors."

"We swear."

"He give me twenty bucks. I give him the key to Six W. It's like you said, a reserve room. We don' let it out ever in case somebody important shows up without a reservation and hasta have a room and we're full up."

"We know," said Horne.

"Six W. I can getcha the key if you wanta see it. You wanta see it?"

"It's not necessary," said Horne, exchanging glances with Perry.

"Is that all?"

Herbert's hand started for the three ten-dollar bills. Perry swept them out of his reach and restored them to his wallet.

"Hey!"

"Hey, what?"

"I tolja whatcha wanted to know. Gimme my money."

"*Your* money?"

"You laid it out."

"So I did, son, but only to examine it." Perry clapped an appreciative hand to Herbert's shoulder. "Much obliged for the information. You have yourself a pleasant day."

They stood outside the hotel. Horne lit a Jersey cheroot and pulled on it thoughtfully.

"There's no point in searching Six W, of course," Perry murmured.

"He's on his way back to Skagway. What time is it?"

"I've got nine-fifty. T.G.—"

"Let's go over to the docks."

"Oh no you don't! No, I don't. I'm not going back to that awful place—not on your life, not for a million in gold coins. And you're crazy if you do."

"That's where he's heading, no doubt with murder in his heart. If he's successful, Marion'll never see an alienist, much less the inside of an asylum. We've got to get moving. Come on."

"I'm not coming. Must I spell it out on a signboard? Imbecile! Stubborn jackass! Damn you!"

"What are you getting so hot about? Where are you going?"

Perry had begun to back away for him, pushing sight of him clear with upraised hand. Anyone passing by would have imagined Horne to be afflicted with some loathsome communicable disease.

"I'm going back to Texas."

"I'll meet you in San Antonio. Keep a chair open for me."

"I don't care; I'm finished caring. I . . ." Perry dropped his hands. He looked suddenly sheepish and at the same time continuing upset. The two expressions clashed on his handsome face. "Ahem, there's just one thing. I'll need a few dollars. A thousand'll do, just to tide me over."

"*You* want to borrow from *me?*"

"Oh, stop it! An ordinary loan. I don't hesitate to loan you money."

"At fifty-percent interest."

"You wouldn't charge me such a rate. That's usury!"

"That's your rate. A thousand dollars, fifty-percent interest compounded daily."

"Bloodsucker! Ingrate! After all I've done, even to risking my life for you and your wild-goose chase. Have you no shame?"

All this was vociferously uttered with his hand held forth expectantly. Ignoring the tirade, Horne counted out a thousand. Perry jammed it in his pocket, and glared fiercely, ferociously. It was all Horne could do to keep from laughing. Perry saw and avoided further embarrassment by retreating, whirling about, and stomping off.

"Good-bye, Mr. Youngquist, sir. Pleasure doing business with you. See you in San Antonio. And don't forget, that's fifty-percent interest compounded daily."

20

Over a thousand miles to Skagway. Horne was beginning to feel like a homing pigeon; whenever he got away from the place, Lucien pulled him back. And he had no choice in the matter. Lucien was definitely heading there, bringing his wealth and the jewelry with him.

He speculated on what was in the Frenchman's mind. Did he believe he'd won the battle of wits at last, had succeeded in convincing Horne that he no longer had either the sixty thousand or the trinkets? Would *he*, Horne wondered, think he'd finally outfoxed him, were the shoe on the other foot? It was hard to say and actually not all that important, apart from the fact that Horne's arrival in Skagway would surprise Lucien if indeed he had decided he'd won. Maybe they'd end up shooting it out. Horne wasn't at all sure he could shoot him; he could hit him over the head or smack him in the jaw hard enough to distribute his habitual smirk all over his face, but kill him?

Lucien had no such reservations concerning Marion. Clearly, he loved his brother much more than he did her. He probably had no feeling for her, only pretending to reciprocate her devotion. Such was not an uncommon relationship, with all the love on one side and the other simply taking advantage of the arrangement, getting what he or she could get out of it before it soured or otherwise ended, before the straying wife murdered the unknowing husband.

Did Louis have any idea what was going on behind his back? Probably not. What punishment his self-respect would have incurred! And his love for Lucien would have suffered irreparable damage.

No, they'd kept their secret from him while she continued to play the devoted wife, at least in public. What sort of marriage had they had behind closed doors? he wondered. No marriage, not the shadow of pretense. Infatuated as she was with Lucien, she had to loathe Louis. She'd murdered him in cold blood. She'd been the only one armed—John Meriweather made no mention of any gun near Louis—and how she'd shot him was interesting. People don't generally shoot their victims in the head at close range. People die just as easily shot in the heart. Her shooting Louis in the head said something eloquent about her feeling for him.

Had she asked him for a divorce and been turned down? That could be. That, combined with her frustration with him, the absence of love, and her infatuation with Lucien, provided all the motivation she needed. From the way Meriweather described his arresting her— her admission that she was planning to run off to Anchorage, her willingness to accompany him to jail without protest, her admitting the deed—it was almost as if she no longer cared. It was all over, the thorn removed from her side. She was indifferent to the consequences of her actions. The only thing that had upset her was Meriweather's telling her Lucien was on his way south instead of toward Anchorage. She had refused to believe it at first, but when he convinced her it was true, only then did she break down. Fortunately for him, he had had the good sense to wait until she was locked up before springing it on her. Whereupon, as he must have expected, she went wild.

The expression on Lucien's face when he stopped resisting and accepted the news of Louis' death had been priceless. If a brain wave could wing its way to

Skagway and strangle her in her cell, she would be
dead and buried before he even stepped off the boat.
That he had no real use for her, possibly even when
making love to her, disliking her intensely for cheating
on his beloved brother, was probably the case. Still,
Horne couldn't believe he wanted her dead. She may
have been the nuisance all clinging vines are. Her
falling all over him could have irritated him, but that
was a small price to pay for the enjoyable rompings she
gave him and the pedestal she put him on. His ego had
to revel in that alone. What man doesn't enjoy owning a
love slave?

Now he was on his way home to murder her. What a
switch! Only if he succeeded and got away, it would be
for good. If he failed to, if Meriweather apprehended
him, Horne could visit him in jail, maybe even testify
at his trial, describe for the prosecution Lucien's reaction when told the bad news, his threat to strangle her.

It was funny, even remarkable, how situations that
you think have complicated themselves to the absolute
limit prove you wrong and go on getting hairier by the
hour.

He paid for his passage and was on board the *Elinor
Sellers* bound for Juneau and Skagway at eleven-twenty-
three. Only one packet had preceded their departure,
none other than the *Charles E. Sterling*. Captain
Bairsford had taken on a cargo of rice and flour, mail,
and several passengers at seven-thirty. As usual, as had
become habitual, Horne found himself precious hours
behind his quarry.

The *Elinor Sellers* was only a year in service, according to one of his fellow passengers, a drummer from
Portland who made a trip "thirty or forty times a year."
His name was Bancroft, originally from Omaha, he was
a handsome, windy sort who less than two minutes into
their acquaintanceship, formed at the railing, confessed
to having a wife and two children in Portland and a wife
and three children in Juneau. Horne was curious as to

how a shoe, boot, belt, and gaiter salesman managed to support two families on what had to be a fairly unimpressive income. But he was not curious enough to put the question to Bancroft. And Bancroft had no interest in elaborating on either of his broods, preferring instead to show of his knowledge of the *Elinor Sellers*.

"Her hull was built by William Campbell Sons' S. and E. B. Company of Philadelphia. She's two hundred and six feet long by thirty-five wide at her beam and nineteen deep. She has one compound engine with cylinders of twenty-four inches and thirty-eighty inches by thirty-six stroke. I love engine specifications, fascinating field of study."

Horne was less than fascinated in who had built her, how big she was, what propelled her, or any other of her vital statistics. His chief and only concerns were that she continue to float and get them to Skagway with all possible speed. So intent was he on getting there, he stood for over an hour at the railing, pretending to listen to Bancroft's story of his life, silently and physically—hunching his shoulders slightly bowing his neck—urging the vessel forward.

Morning gave way to afternoon. The sky was a pristine blue, cloudless, the breeze refreshing, the sea unusually calm. A poker game began in the main cabin. Bancroft invited him to join with him.

"I have to warn you, though, I'm experienced. I sure get to play enough—win, too. I won forty dollars coming down from Juneau last trip. Fifty-cent limit; winning that much in less than two hours takes some skill, I don't mind telling you. You play much?"

"Not much."

"Then maybe you're right to stay out. There's cardsharps all over these boats like barnacles. Fellow has to keep a weather eye out. I sit on my wallet when I play. Can't be too careful when there's strangers and money involved. Hey, why don't you just come down and watch? You know, kibitz."

Horne agreed to. He stood by as Bancroft bought

and stacked his chips and positioned himself behind
him so he could see his cards. In the very first hand,
straight draw, he pulled three kings. He bet them like
they were a royal flush, driving everybody else out
almost at once. And raked in the pot happily.

"How do you like that for starters?" he crowed to
Horne.

"Wonderful."

Great, Marvelous. Played like a true professional.
Pull your cards, throw your money at the pot, drive
everybody to cover, wind up with the antes and your
own uncalled bet. When, had he played his hand with
restraint, with patience and intelligence, he could have
kept others in the hand, would have ended up winning,
possibly even with kings full, although three kings alone
is powerful enough to win three hands out of four in
draw.

He drew next to no cards in the five hands that
followed—in two of the five not even a pair—but he
doggedly stayed, losing his ante and first go-round bet.
Then his luck changed dramatically. Throughout the
ensuing two hours practically every other hand saw him
draw good to excellent cards. With them, playing rashly,
thoughtlessly, often stupidly, he won.

But only a fraction of what he could and should have.

Horne stood watching in amazement. The exhibition
could only be described as a lesson, a primer in practice
of how not to play poker. Horne did not comment, did
not alter his expression, affected no outward sign of
disapproval, uncomfortableness, or frustration. Bancroft's
mistakes were not as blatant as his initial one, when he
drew three kings and promptly scared everyone out
before they could contribute to the pot. For example,
he drew queens up and, although sitting to the left of
the opener, did not raise. Queens up can be beaten if
too many players stay; so, if four or more of the seven
stay after the pot is opened, the queens up is worth a
call but not a raise. In such a situation strong players
may fold, but once a poor player decides to stay, it's

hard to drive him out. In a nutshell, if you have jacks up, queens up, kings or aces up and you're sitting to the opener's left, raise. If you're raised back, fold or reraise and stand pat. In the latter case, you have to bet after the draw and hope the other fellow doesn't call, because his raise before the draw probably means he can beat your two pair.

If in the same situation you're holding a small pair, fold. They're simply not worth playing unless you raise before the draw and stand pat, then bet. It's eleven to one you won't make a full house.

From long and astute observation of opponents' failings and strengths, idiosyncracies and habits, Horne had come to agree with Perry's conclusion: "three out of four of all poker players are simpletons." Bancroft played like a simpleton. Another player would open; even a simpleton should realize that the opener is holding at least a pair of jacks, but the simpleton will stay with a small pair. All one has to do is count the players to stay in when a pot is opened. In a seven-handed game there will be about three pairs distributed among the players on average, possibly a four-card straight or flush and an inside straight. Four or even five players will ordinarily stay with not one of them holding, on average, better than two jacks.

Why draw to an inside straight? It's eleven to one you won't make it. A four-card flush or four-card straight should never be played unless there is five times as much money in the pot as the bet itself.

But the first rule, the one that should be permanently burned into every player's brain, is: never stay with a small pair.

Never stay with less than two aces or two kings.

If you have three of a kind above tens, don't raise. Bancroft had three kings, raised, and drove everybody out. You want the other players in.

If your three of a kind are below tens, raise. Because you don't want too many drawing against you. One interesting thing about three cards that Perry had taught

Horne: your chances of drawing another pair if you draw three are greatly enhanced because the cards are very often not too well shuffled and the pairs tend to stick together from the deal before.

Most mediocre players are in too much of a hurry to open. If you're sitting close to the dealer's left, don't be in a rush. If you have a strong hand and someone ahead of you looks like he's going to open, pass, and raise when it comes back to you. And the opposite, if you have only aces or kings. Open as soon as you can if you see too many players preparing to toss in their hands.

A good poker player takes the time and makes the effort to learn the game. A poor player, playing poorly his whole life, doesn't know what a good hand is and doesn't know how to play it if he catches it. Such a player was Bancroft. The sole factor that was preventing him from losing his shirt, the thing that was to, surprisingly, almost guarantee that he'd come out slightly ahead, was that the other participants were no better players than he. A couple were worse. In a sequence of five hands one man drew two inside straights in three of them. And of course lost. And of course lamented his "bad luck" and took solace in the others' sympathetic pronouncements. Horne was very tempted to tell him he deserved to lose, was an idiot to play such hands, but it was none of his business.

God bless and keep such people, he reflected. Without them people like him would have to turn to legitimate ways of making a living. Compete with their equals and betters instead of enjoying the luxury of fleecing the Bancrofts of this world.

Bancroft dropped out of a hand, discarding four cards of an inside straight, much to Horne's surprise.

"I don't draw to inside straights," he explained. "Not unless I'm red-hot."

"Good thinking," said Horne.

Bancroft was counting his chips. "I'm about thirty-five ahead," he whispered.

"Good."

"Say, you must be getting tired standing on your feet watching. Next time a seat opens up, why don't you take it?"

Why don't you? asked two of the others with their eyes.

"I don't think so," said Horne. "I don't think I can keep up with you boys."

"You keep watching, you'll be surprised how quick you can pick up the finer points, the little tricks that separate the men from the boys."

Five-card draw, deuces wild with the joker, was called for. The hand was played to completion. Horne assessed everyone's strength and strategy. Bancroft had opened with a pair of aces. The player to his left had stayed with two queens. A sure way to go broke. The next player raised with three aces. The fourth, fifth, and sixth players folded. The seventh called with three jacks, not particularly shrewd. Bancroft stayed with his two aces, sending good money after bad. The holder of the two queens also called. Horne sighed, reflecting on the folly of man.

After the draw Bancroft came up with an ace-high straight. The holder of the queens failed to better them. The holder of the three aces drew two cards, one another ace. The holder of the jacks drew two cards and failed to better them.

Bancroft checked his ace-high straight. The queens checked. The four aces bet. The three jacks folded. Bancroft called, the queens folded, the aces won.

Bancroft's reaction was not that of a poor loser, only mild disappointment at "being outdrawn." Horne didn't have the heart to tell him that he'd been beaten before the first bet. And so it went. Bancroft won, he lost, he threw his money into a losing hand, others threw theirs into losing hands, making him a winner, almost as if by default. It was the sloppiest, most amateurish, blunder-filled game of poker Horne had ever kibitzed. It was a capable player's nightmare, a debacle. It boggled the mind. A rousing good time was being had by all. The game was still in progress when a shout went up outside the cabin door.

"Storm dead ahead!"

The reaction was neither as sudden nor as vigorus as that Horne had witnessed on board the *Charles E. Sterling* when someone shouted fire, but it was enough to end the game. The players cashed in their chips, put on their jackets, and counting their money, streamed out onto the deck with the kibitzers. The vessel had only moments before passed Cape Flattery. Vancouver Island was on their right. Nightfall was about two hours ahead. The sky, which had been uniformly bright blue and cloudless earlier, had assumed a pattern of varying shades of gray. Dead ahead the oncoming storm dropped straight down. The water was getting choppier by the minute. As Horne watched fascinated, the flow of the vessel began wandering to starboard, suggesting that the captain was attempting to avoid the full force of the monster by closing on shore. Horne had heard that all along the West Coast the waters were rocky and treacherous to about a quarter-mile out. This meant the vessel could not venture too close to the effort to skirt the storm. A trap between a rock and a hard place threatened.

Nearer and nearer drew the storm. It too appeared to be moving toward the shoreline. The captain and steersman took note and eased the bow back to port intending, it appeared, to meet the monster head-on.

"We're bulling straight into her," exclaimed Bancroft behind him, forced to raise his voice above the rising wind to be heard.

"Isn't that the worst thing we can do?"

"No choice. We're already too close. Trying to turn away this close, we'd get smacked broadside, tip over. Straight to Davy Jones' locker, all hands lost."

He grinned. Horne failed to see the humor. Bancroft retreated from it.

"It'll be okay, you'll see. I've been through worse

than this, haven't gone down yet. Don't plan to go down now."

Again he grinned. Horne suddenly didn't like him. How, he wondered, could Brancroft tell at a distance how bad this one was? T.G. gripped the railing with both hands, his fingers aching, his knuckles pure white, as the vanguard winds of the storm began to blow up viciously. The boat began to stagger as the seas heaved. The wind rose to a higher and higher scream as it raked the ship; the sea churned, boiling white, heaving and writhing around them as if lifting in response to a series of subterranean explosions. The fist of fear clutched Horne's throat.

A voice shouted above the gale. "Everybody inside! Inside! Everybody!"

All obeyed except two of the card players who seemed to be mesmerized by sight of the approaching storm. They had to be pulled from the railing and bustled into the main cabin.

The wind shrieked above their heads, the cabin rocked, chairs and the table slid about, men sought to hold themselves upright by grasping anything solid within reach, some failing to, falling, sliding across the heaving floor. The boat rolled and plunged, and staggered and lurched as the black menace struck in all its fury, engorging the *Elinor Sellers*.

Horne clamped his eyes shut, held his breath, gripped the brass railing alongside the door, and thought about death. He had never been caught in a storm at sea before; he almost never traveled by sea, not even coasting. It was a new and terrifying, dreadful experience, mainly because he felt so utterly helpless, stripped completely of control over his fate. This was no place for a human, he mused; cliffs, rocks, even trees can contend with such terrible punishment, but not the frail vessel that is the human body. In the wrong place at the wrong time, unequipped to deal was what he, what they all were. It was unfair, it was wrong. He hadn't maneuvered the packet to that place at that time, hadn't tried to avoid the storm, changed his mind, and headed her into it. He wasn't even permitted to steer, to exercise his judgment; his life was in the hands of someone at the wheel he'd never even seen, who'd never seen him.

"We'll never make it," he muttered. "We're heading for the bottom."

"We'll make it," said Bancroft almost jauntily. "It can't keep up but a few minutes more. We've got to be two-thirds through it by now. This ship is new, solidly built, steel, not old, dried timbers. We're sitting low on the sea, not poking up, no masts to topple and come crashing down. We'll make it, we'll make it."

Oh, shut up with your stupid optimism, thought Horne. Shut up, period. Anybody who plays poker the way you do doesn't know anything about anything!

Through the storm they nosed, floundering and pitching forward out of her fury, the churning water flaying the hull, waves punishing, gale ripping at the deck and superstructure, helm up and down, up and down, until they were clear, and in seconds the sea settled, the vessel came to level and held it. On they steamed.

"You're white as a sheet," said Bancroft good-naturedly. "Am I?"

He was not; his complexion had not changed in the slightest; he hadn't been at all nervous, not a single worried look, not a serious concern from when the storm was first sighted to now. But there was an explanation for all of it, decided Horne; it's a known fact that experiences terrifying to normal people and the other higher animals have little or no effect on imbeciles.

The *Elinor Sellers* had suffered little damage; Horne's heart resumed beating normally and the poker game continued. Horne avoided it, going to his cabin and lying down in hopes of completing his recovery from the ordeal.

Two days later they stopped off at Juneau to unload

some of their cargo and a handful of passengers. Horne
stood at the railing thinking about the trial, the after-
math, Perry's taking up with Agatha Trent Woodward.
It all seemed as if it had happened ten years ago. He
wondered about Agatha and how she had taken Perry's
deserting her. It was no way to treat a lady, but the way
the lady had been treating him had him frightfully worried about his elderly life and fragile limbs. Horne
couldn't fault him for escaping.

The *Elinor Sellers* made its way much too slowly up
the Lynn Canal. T.G.'s thoughts flew ahead of her bow.
It would all finally come to its end in Skagway—fittingly.
He wondered what had happened to Marion in his
absence. Was she still in jail or had they removed her
to an institution? If the latter, Lucien might have trouble getting at her. Visitors to mental hospitals weren't
usually permitted to bring guns in with them. Then,
too, usually only the immediate family was encouraged
to visit. Still, Horne could not think of anyone more
resourceful than Lucien. Being as unethical and im-
moral as he was by nature helped greatly in that regard.
Horne did feel sincerely sorry for Marion, as he would
for anyone not responsible for irresponsible bloody acts.
He hoped Lucien wouldn't get to her before he could
get to Lucien. If he did catch up with him in time, he'd
tip off Meriweather; he in turn would alert the asylum.

What asylum? Who said she'd been put in one?

For some reason he couldn't put his finger on, he
felt more confident of success going after Lucien this
time. Probably because John Meriweather would be
handy if he needed help. And he would help him in any
way legal that didn't compromise his authority. Good
man, John.

One thing was in his favor. Lucien would probably
be taking it for granted that his two key scam had
worked, so he wouldn't be expecting him to show up in
Skagway. On the other hand, Lucien did know that
T.G. knew where he was heading, having practically
sent him there. Who could say what beliefs and certainties

lurked in that devious mind? What backup plan he'd come up with for holding him off? Whatever it was, it wouldn't work.

Horne continued to wax optimistic, standing at the railing in the bright sunlight, looking at he snowy mounts, the steep timbered slopes, the birds in endless variety wheeling and diving, and the glacier. Once he got his money, stickpin, and watch back, he'd head south again. He could be in San Antonio in less than a week.

21

He liked San Antonio. Unlike Waco, Dodge, and Deadwood, it was a quiet town, almost sleepy, the people friendly, troublemakers in small supply, the area stepped in fascinating history. The last time there he had visited the Alamo and communed with the ghosts of the heroic defenders. Best of all, he'd be reunited with Perry. Perry would have rethickened his wallet by the time he arrived and be able to repay the thousand at 50 percent compound interest. There was wealth in San Antonio area. They would play and win, and life in general would be restored to something like normalcy.

He would never come back to Skagway or even Alaska. It was still a little too rough for his taste. He wasn't as paranoid about Skagway as Perry, but having already seen it, he knew he'd have no desire to revisit.

The *Elinor Sellers* dropped anchor in almost the identical spot where the *Charles E. Sterling* stopped on their first visit. The ferry approached, everyone disembarked. Horne saw no sign of Bancroft, recalled he had a wife and family in Juneau, and had doubtless gotten off there. Since the storm two days before, Horne had avoided him; knowing that Bancroft would have no trouble striking up a new acquaintanceship.

Nudging the top of the shallow harbor before it, the ferry approached the docks. The lines were thrown and made fast, the passengers and their luggage transferred

186

to the dock. Bag in hand, .45 on his hip, .22 Sharps in its little holster at the small of his back, Barns .50 in its leg holster, dagger-mounted knuckle-duster in his inside pocket, Horne started for Broadway Street. Four men sat about on packing cases talking. He was passing them, picking up his pace, eager to get to John Meriweather's, when one of the speakers halted him in his tracks.

"Didn' ya here? The *Charles E. Sterling*. Went to the bottom in a storm offn' Capt Scott."

Horne stiffened.

"Excuse me, did I hear you say the *Charles E. Sterling*?"

"That's right," said another man. "Sank with all hands an' passengers."

"Not all," corrected a third man. "They was some s'vivors."

"Abner's right. 'Swhat I heerd," said a fourth. "They was a fishin' smack takin' salmon close by. Runned for the cape and made it to shelter 'fore the wust of it hit. Bastard storm come whirlin' down from the gulf like a tornado."

"Mir'cle they wasn't more'n the one ship to go to the bottom," said the first man.

Said the fourth, "One o' the boys 'board the fisherman was Paddy Scanlon's cousin Mickey. He had him a ringside seat. Tol' me an' Paddy it was terrifyin' to behold. The sea churned up white far as the eye could see like a blanket o' snow 'cross the Kansas plains. The *Charles E.* didn' seem to know which way to turn to 'void it. Ended up turnin' out to sea, Chrissakes, which hadda be the wust thing she coulda."

Abner nodded. "She caught the full brunt o' it broadside, I heered, turned over like a cup, wallowed upside down for a bit, then down went her stern, pulling her to the bottom."

"They say the water's only a quarter-mile deep off Cape Scott," said the first man.

"Deep 'nough to drown in," said another. "Bucket's

deep 'nough to drown in if ya' wanna' end it all. That's how Elmer Scoggins killed hisself."

"My God," murmured Horne. "Did I hear you say there were four survivors?"

"More'n that," said the third speaker. "Maybe 'leven or twelve, only by the time the fishin' smack was able to reach 'em, most had drownded. They pulled five out, one died on the way in; others come out okay. All four was crew."

"No passengers."

"Nary a one."

Horne thanked them and went on his way. The *Charles E. Sterling*, Captain Bairsford, Lucien DeBlois, at the bottom off Queen Charlotte Strait. The same storm that had struck the *Elinor Sellers*. And survival and failure to had come down to steering. Their captain had headed into the storm; Bairsford, apparently after some indecision, headed out to sea, exposing his starboard beam.

Sending Lucien, his $60,040, his precious diamond horseshoe stickpin, his beloved thousand-dollar Jürgensen watch with the one-carat diamond set in the stem to the bottom. He felt a sudden impulse to curse wildly, but immediately decided it would be entirely inappropriate to a catastrophe of such magnitude.

Gone. Forever. Every penny, every diamond, every notched wheel and tiny spring, the proud and gleaming gold case, artistically crafted face, slender hands, fifty-two-link chain.

To his dismay as he trudged along, his shoulders sagging, his entire body drooping and losing energy at a rapid rate, he became aware of tears in his eyes.

Marion DeBlois had come narrowly close to fulfilling Lucien's plans for her. She tired to kill herself; she sharpened the lip of her spoon—held back when her supper dishes were picked up two nights before—on the stone floor of her cell and slashed her wrists. Luckily, John Meriweather got to her in time, knocked her cold, and bandaged the damage. The morning of the day before Horne arrived two alienists called on her and came away in agreement that she was mentally deranged and should be removed as soon as possible to an institution.

"This morning bright and early two orderlies and a lady doctor came from the asylum in Juneau and took her off my hands, thank the Lord."

Meriweather sat with his feet up on his desk. He looked to Horne a trifle ragged around the edges; lodging this particular prisoner must have been something of an ordeal.

"You should have been here," he went on.

"I'm glad I wasn't."

"Should have heard her, the way she twisted everything. Up until the minute she left she insisted Lucien would be coming back for her."

"Oh, he was coming back, all right."

"He wouldn't have gotten near her. Anyway, he was coming back, they'd be reunited and live happily ever after, I guess. And with Louis' blessing."

"Wasn't she overlooking something?"

"She had him still alive. She hadn't shot him, hadn't looted the safe. Never went near the store that night. And she and Louis had a long talk about their marriage and agreed there was no future to it and he sportingly announced that he'd step aside in favor of Lucien."

"Talk about brotherly love."

"She told him all this as calmly and coherently as you please. The one I feel sorry for is her father."

"Did he come to see her?"

"Just once. Only stayed a few minutes. Poor man couldn't take it. When he came back out here, he was crying like a baby. What a mess, what a tragedy; both brothers dead, the wife insane, the old man left alone. My impression is he's pretty helpless without her." He paused. "Sorry to hear about your money and things."

"*You're* sorry?"

"It may not help any, probably won't, but there is a little consolation. Very little.

"What it is, I'll welcome it."

"You lost it all, he took it all, you're still without it, but so is he. It has to be a little easier to take knowing nobody's got it, least of all the culprit, isn't it? Also, for all the trouble he caused you, he wound up paying as dearly as anyone can, right?"

"I guess."

"Are you going back right away?"

"On the boat I came up on. She's leaving in about thirty minutes."

"That was short and sweet."

Both had risen from their chairs. They shook hands.

"Think you'll ever be back up this way?"

"Never."

Meriweather chuckled. "Alaska's not your style; you could call it the rough neck of the woods. You're too civilized for us, T.G."

"No more civilized than you."

"Oh, hell, I was born here. It all comes natural to me. I'll live my life and die and never leave. But that's all right. Say hello to Mr. Youngquist for me, and good luck at the table."

Horne paused outside the office long enough to light his last Jersey cheroot, then started for the docks and the waiting ferry. On the way down the coast as they were passing Cape Scott, the engineer drew everyone's attention to a spot off their starboard.

"Right there's where the *Charles E. Sterling* went down the other day," he announced.

Horne stared at the water and closed his eyes. And saw something round and gold shimmering as the clear water passed over it. He sighed, shook his head, and walked away from the railing.